REAL LOSSES,
IMAGINARY GAINS

Books by Wright Morris

Novels

A LIFE

WAR GAMES

FIRE SERMON

IN ORBIT

ONE DAY

CAUSE FOR WONDER

WHAT A WAY TO GO

CEREMONY IN LONE TREE

LOVE AMONG THE CANNIBALS

THE FIELD OF VISION

THE HUGE SEASON

THE DEEP SLEEP

THE WORKS OF LOVE

MAN AND BOY

THE WORLD IN THE ATTIC

THE MAN WHO WAS THERE

MY UNCLE DUDLEY

Photo-Text

LOVE AFFAIR: A VENETIAN JOURNAL

GOD'S COUNTRY AND MY PEOPLE

THE HOME PLACE

THE INHABITANTS

Essays

ABOUT FICTION

A BILL OF RITES, A BILL OF WRONGS, A BILL OF GOODS

THE TERRITORY AHEAD

Anthology

WRIGHT MORRIS: A READER

Short Stories

REAL LOSSES, IMAGINARY GAINS

REAL LOSSES, IMAGINARY GAINS

Wright Morris

HARPER & ROW, PUBLISHERS

New York,
Hagerstown,
San Francisco,
London

"Green Grass, Blue Sky, White House," "A Fight Between a White Boy and a Black Boy in the Dusk of a Fall Afternoon in Omaha, Nebraska," "Here Is Einbaum," "Real Losses, Imaginary Gains" originally appeared in *The New Yorker*; "Fiona," "Drrdla," in *Esquire*; "Since When Do They Charge Admission" in *Harper's Magazine*; "In Another Country" in *The Atlantic Monthly*; "Magic" in *The Southern Review*; "The Safe Place" in *The Kenyon Review*; "The Ram in the Thicket" in *Harpers Bazaar* (both published in *Wright Morris: A Reader*, Harper & Row, Publishers, Inc.); "The Rites of Spring" in *New World Writing*; "The Cat's Meow" was originally published by Black Sparrow Press, Los Angeles.

FIRST EDITION

Designed by Gloria Adelson

Library of Congress Cataloging in Publication Data

Morris, Wright, date
  Real losses, imaginary gains.
  CONTENTS: Real losses, imaginary gains.—Since when do they charge admission.—The ram in the thicket.—Here is Einbaum. [etc.]
  I. Title.
PZ3.M8346Re   [PS3525.O7475]   813'.5'2   75–33473
ISBN 0–06–013098–9

Contents

For Virginia and Bernice

Real Losses, Imaginary Gains

On the firm's stationery, the loose pages in disorder, sent off to me by regular mail to a previous address, my cousin Daniel writes me that our Aunt Winona has passed away. A blow to us all. A loss that found him unprepared. Among her meager effects, stored away in its box, he found the silk kimono he had brought her from Hong Kong. Money given to her she sent to missionaries. He writes me in longhand, filling the margins, using both sides of the paper, giving vent to his affection, his frustration, his helplessness. In the past he only wrote such letters to her.

I see by the date it is more than three weeks since she passed away. My father's people, protesting but resigned, still reluctantly die, or go to their reward, but my mother's four sisters have all passed away. The phrase is accurate, and I use it out of respect for the facts.

Last summer we stopped in Boise to see her, the house both crushed and supported by huge bushes of lilacs. When I put my arms around her she said, "There's nothing much to me, is there?" One day she would say, "Let me just rest a moment," and pass away.

My aunt's couch faced the door, which stood open, the view given a sepia tone by the rusted screen. At the bottom, where children sometimes leaned, it bulged inward to shape a small hole. The view framed by the door was narrow if seen from the couch. Lying there, my aunt took in only what was passing: she did not see what approached, or how it slipped away. On the steps of the bungalow across the street children often crouched, listening to summer. In the yard a knotted rope dangled a tire swing to where it had swept away the grass. A car passed, a stroller passed, music from somewhere hovered and passed, hours and days, weeks and months, spring to winter and back to spring, war and peace, affluence and depression, loved ones, old ones, good ones and bad ones, all passed away.

"Who is that?" she asked, as the picture framed by the door altered. My aunt lay on the couch, I was seated on the ottoman at her side. We were able to share the sunlit picture and the wavering shadow it cast toward the porch. The glare of light penetrated the sleeves of an elderly lady's blouse, and took an X-ray impression of her bloomers. Perhaps my aunt knew her. Had she stopped to admire the flowering lilac, or tactfully attract my aunt's attention? Her quandary had about it something vaguely imploring, of a person hopefully expectant. If her presence in the picture gave it a moral, the word "losses" gave it an appropriate caption. Just losses, not specifying what they were.

My aunt lifted her head to call out, "Would you like to step in?" Over the years, over the decades, many people had. The very young had given way to the very old, defying all belief that they had ever been children. Perplexities of this sort might lead my aunt to place her face in her hands, as if weeping. What she hoped to contain was her laughter, not at all that of an elderly, religious woman. On my father's side all of my Protestant aunts shared a common ceremony to ease the pain of this world, uttering no word as they gathered their aprons to hurl them like tent flaps over their heads. My Aunt Winona laughed: one might think it the muffled mirth of a child. Her nephews and nieces, the offspring of God-fearing parents, had grown up to be thrice married or worse, and divorced, their belief limited to one remaining article of Faith—that *she* would understand. She did not understand, not for a moment, but their belief released the resources of her forgiveness, and gave proven sinners three to four times their share of her concern and love.

Perhaps the woman in the picture, poised like a worming robin, sensed the presence of strangers. She wheeled slowly, her dangling bag brushing the tops of the uncut grass. Her bearings taken, she went off in the direction from which she had come. The picture framed by the door, empty of its previous meaning, called to my attention the loose, dangerous boards of the porch. On the lower stoop one was curled like a ski tip. Over the years these boards had been mentioned, or were invisibly present, in much of my aunt's correspondence. One of her nephews always planned to do something about them. Recently, however—in the last twenty years—they have paid her only brief, flying visits, in which there was no time to be wasted repairing porches. Also, it was the porch itself now, not a few boards, that needed to be replaced. That would require removing the ambush of lilacs, replacing both the porch roof and one wall of the house. The floor in the bathroom tilted in a manner that delayed draining the tub. A late addition to the house, it had a self-opening door, and guests had to be warned.

On our arrival we had been given glasses of well water for refreshment. It was water but resembled broth in which life was emerging. About water she was eccentric. It was her opinion that water out of pipes lay at the root of many disorders, including some of her own. Well water, however, cleansed the system of its poisons. Water coursing through miles of pipes picked up poisons. This water came from the well of a friend, who brought it to her weekly, in gallon-size vinegar bottles. From there it was poured into mayonnaise jars and stored on the bottom shelf of the refrigerator. This shelf was cool but not cold: one might as well eat raw potatoes as pour ice-cold water on the stomach. After this water had sat for a spell, cooling, a sediment collected on the jar's bottom. Pouring the water from the jar into a glass stirred it up, so that the varieties of life could be studied. My wife had seen things swimming. I searched it for some sign of polliwogs.

The windows of the house were cluttered with plants that filtered the light like cataracts. Posses of flies had their own territories, and staged raiding parties. A fly swatter was used to break up these games if they got too rough. On the wall beside the couch, tucked into a loose strip of molding, were postcards from her far-flung friends. One from Perth, Australia, featured a baby kangaroo peering from its mother's pouch. There were numberless cards of kittens playing with balls of yarn, kittens stuffed into baskets, kittens asleep with puppies. Postcards from faraway places were not unusual, with so many of her friends being missionaries of the Adventist faith.

With her father and sisters—the sisters could be seen in a photo on the bric-a-brac shelf behind her—Aunt Winona had left the plains at the turn of the century to settle on a homestead near Boise, Idaho. Her father felt the plains of Nebraska were getting crowded, and moved his family of daughters westward. The two sons had already taken off on their own. Her father and mother were shown in a photo taken in the salon in Grand Island, Nebraska, in 1884. Her father is seated, and her mother stands at his side, her right hand resting on his left shoulder, more of a bride in appearance than the pioneer mother of seven children. The husband is holding the new child in the cradle of his arm. This child is my mother. She will die within a few days of my birth.

I was a young man of nineteen before I set eyes on my aunt and other members of my mother's family. I came west from Chicago, my locker covered with the stickers of Ivy League colleges I hoped to go to. I wore a blue serge suit and my pair of Paris garters. My grandfather was old but spry, a God-fearing man long prepared for God. I saw him in the flickering glow of kerosene lamps, a second-time child to his matronly daughters. Only my mother was missing: he searched my face to recoup that loss. I slept that night in a large bed with two uncles, who assured me that my lack of Adventist faith was not crucial. The love of my aunts would be more than enough to get me into Heaven, if that was my wish.

In the morning my Aunt Winona, the only one not to marry, stood in the sunlit kitchen and watched me eat. Her first love had been the Lord, the second her father, and in this world she had found no replacement. It was him she saw when she gazed at me. She gave to this farmhouse kitchen, the light flaming her hair, the time-stopped dazzle of Vermeer's paintings. She poured milk from a bowl, threaded a needle, picked up crumbs from the table with her tip-moistened finger. She was at once serene, vulnerable, and unshakable. The appalling facts of this world existed to be forgiven. In her presence I was subject to fevers of faith, to fits of stark belief. Like the grandfather, she saw me as a preacher in search of a flock.

In a recent letter she wrote:

> When your mother died my sister Violet, who was married, wanted to take you, but your father would not consent to it. He said, "He is all I have left of Grace." O dear boy, you were the center of so much suffering, so many losses you will never know, realize, or feel . . .

What is it I feel now, sitting here in the full knowledge of my loss? In my mind's eye I see her couch, now empty, the impression of her figure like that the wind leaves on tall grass.

No, in the flesh there was nothing much to her—she had reduced the terms by which we measure real gains and losses. "I always thought she needed me," her nephew wrote, "and now I find I'm the one who needs her." That's a miserable loss. I weigh mine each time I lift a glass of water and note its temperature, its color, and what it is that swims I can no longer see.

1973

Since When Do They Charge Admission

On the morning they left Kansas, May had tuned in for the weather and heard of the earthquake in San Francisco, where her daughter, Janice, was seven months pregnant. So she had called her. Her husband, Vernon Dickey, answered the phone. He was a native Californian so accustomed to earthquakes he thought nothing of them. It was the wind he feared.

"When I read about those twisters," he said to May, "I don't know how you people stand it." He wouldn't believe that May had never seen a twister till she saw one on TV, and that one in Missouri.

"Ask him about the riots," Cliff had asked her.

"What riots, Mrs. Chalmers?"

It was no trouble for May to see that Janice could use someone around the house to talk to. She was like her father, Cliff, in that it took children to draw her out. Her sister, Charlene, would talk the leg off a stranger but the girls had never talked much to each other. But now they would, once the men got out of the house. It had been Cliff's idea to bring Charlene along since she had never been out of Kansas. She had never seen an ocean. She had never been higher than Estes Park.

On their way to the beach, Charlene cried, "Look! Look!" She pointed into the sunlight; May could see the light shimmering on the water.

"That's the beach," said Janice.

"Just *look*," Charlene replied.

"You folks come over here often?" asked Cliff.

"On Vernon's day off," replied Janice.

"If it's a weekday," said May, "you wouldn't find ten people on a beach in Merrick County."

"You wouldn't because there's no beach for them to go to," said Janice.

Cliff liked the way Janice spoke up for California, since that was what she was stuck with. He didn't like it, himself. Nothing had its own place. Hardly any of the corners were square. All through the Sunday morning service he could hear the plastic propellers spinning at the corner gas station, and the loud bang when they checked the oil and slammed down the hood. Vernon Dickey took it all in his stride, the way he did the riots.

Janice said, "Vernon's mother can't understand anybody who lives where they have dust storms."

"I'd rather see it blow than feel it shake," said Cliff.

"Ho-ho!" said Vernon.

"I suppose it's one thing or another," said May.

8

"When I read about India I'm always thankful."

Cliff honked his horn at the sharp turns in the road. The fog stood offshore just far enough to let the sun shine yellow on the beach sand. At the foot of the slope the beach road turned left through a grove of trees. Up ahead of them a chain, stretched between two posts, blocked the road. On the left side a portable contractor's toilet was brightly painted with green and yellow flowers. A cardboard sign attached to the chain read: *Admission 50¢.*

"Since when do they charge admission?" Janice asked. She looked at her husband, a policeman on his day off. As Cliff stopped the car a young man in the booth put out his head.

"In heaven's name," May said. She had never seen a man with such a head of hair outside of *The National Geographic.* He had a beard that seemed to grow from the hair on his chest. A brass padlock joined the ends of a chain around his neck.

"How come the fifty-cent fee?" said Vernon. "It's a public beach."

"It's a racket," said the youth. "You can pay it or not pay it." He didn't seem to care. At his back stood a girl with brown hair to her waist, framing a smiling, vacant, pimpled face. She was eating popcorn; the butter and salt greased her lips.

"I don't know why anyone should pay it," said May. "Cliff, drive ahead."

Cliff said, "You like to lower the chain?"

When the boy stepped from the booth he had nothing on but a jockstrap. The way his plump buttocks were tanned it was plain that was all he was accustomed to wear. He stooped with his backside toward the car, but the hood was between him and the ladies. As the chain slacked Cliff drove over it, slowly, into the parking lot.

"What in the world do you make of *that?*" asked May.

"He's a hippie," said Janice. "They're hippies."

"Now I've finally seen one," said May. She twisted in the seat to take a look back.

"Maybe they're having a love-in down here," said Vernon, and guffawed. Cliff had never met a man with a sense of humor that stayed within bounds.

"Park anywhere," said Janice.

"You come down here alone?" asked May.

Vernon said, "Mrs. Chalmers, you don't need to worry. They're crazy but they're not violent."

Cliff maneuvered between the trucks and cars to where the front wheels thumped against a driftwood log. The sand began there, some of it blowing in the offshore breeze. The tide had washed up a sandbar, just ahead, that concealed the beach and most of the people on it. Way over, maybe five or ten miles, was the coastline just west of the Golden Gate, with the tier on tier of houses that Cliff knew to be Daly City. From the bridge, on the way over, Vernon had pointed it out. Vernon and Janice had a home there, but they wanted something more out in the open, nearer the beach. As a matter of fact, Cliff had come up with the idea of building them something. He was a builder. He and May lived in a house that he had built. If Vernon would come up with the piece of land, Cliff would more or less promise to put a house on it. Vernon would help him on the weekends, and his days off.

"What about a little place over there?" said Cliff, and wagged his finger at the slope near the beach. Right below it were the huge rocks black as the water, but light on their tops. That was gull dung. One day some fellow smarter than the rest would make roof tiles or fertilizer out of it.

"Most of the year it's cold and foggy," said Vernon, "too cold for the kids."

"What good is a cold, windy beach?" said May. She had turned to take the whip of the wind on her back. No one answered her question. It didn't seem the right time to give it much thought. Cliff got the picnic basket out of the rear and tossed the beach blanket to Vernon. There was enough sand in it, when they shook it, to blow back in his face.

"Just like at home," Cliff said to Vernon, who guffawed.

Vernon had been born and raised in California, but he had got his army training near Lubbock, Texas, where the dust still blew. Now he led off toward the beach, walking along the basin left where the tide had receded. Charlene trailed along behind him wearing the flowered pajama suit she had worn since they left Colby, on the fourth of June. They had covered twenty-one hundred and forty-eight miles in five days and half of one night, Cliff at the wheel. Charlene could drive, but May didn't feel she could be trusted on the interstate freeways, where they drove so fast. There was a time, every day, about an hour after lunch, when nothing Cliff could think or do would keep him from dozing off. He'd jerk up when he'd hear the sound of gravel or feel the pull of the wheel on the road's shoulder. Then he'd be good for a few more miles till it happened again. The score of times that happened Cliff might have killed them all but he couldn't bring himself to pull over and stop. It scared him to think of the long drive back.

"Except where it was green, in Utah," said May, "it's looked the same to me since we left home."

"Mrs. Chalmers," said Vernon, "you should've sat on the other side of the car."

It was enlightening to Cliff, after all he'd heard about the population explosion, to see how wide open and empty most of the country was. In the morning he might feel he was all alone in it. The best time of day was the forty miles or so he got in before breakfast. They slipped by so easy he sometimes felt he would just like to drive forever, the women in the car quiet until he stopped for food. Anything May saw before she had her coffee was lost on her. After breakfast Cliff didn't know what seemed longer: the day he put in waiting for the dark, or the long night he put in waiting for the light. He had forgotten about trains until they had to stop for the night.

Vernon said, "I understand that when they take the salt out of the water there'll be no more water problems. Is that right, Mr. Chalmers?"

Like her mother, Charlene said, "There'll just be others." Was there anything Cliff had given these girls besides a poor start? He turned to see how Janice, who was seven months pregnant, was making out. The way her feet had sunk into the sand she was no taller than her mother. With their backsides to the wind both women looked broad as a barn. One day Janice was a girl—the next day you couldn't tell her from her mother. That part of her life that she looked old would prove to be the longest, but seem the shortest. Her mother hardly knew a thing, or cared, about what had happened since the war. The sight of anything aging, or anything just beginning, like that unborn child she was lugging, affected Cliff so strongly he could wet his lips and taste it. Where did people get the strength to do it all over again? He turned back to face the beach and the clumps of people who were sitting around, or lying. One played a guitar. A wood fire smoked in the shelter of a few smooth rocks. Vernon said, "It's like the coast of Spain." Cliff could

12

believe it might well be true: it looked old and bleak enough. Where the sand was wet about half-a-dozen dogs ran up and down, yapping like kids.

"Dogs are fun! They just seem to know almost everything." This side of Charlene made her good with her kids, but Cliff sometimes wondered about her husband.

"How's this?" said Vernon, taking Cliff by the arm, and indicated where he thought they should spread the blanket. On one side were two boys, stretched out on their bellies, and nearer at hand was this blanket-covered figure, his back humped up. His problem seemed to be that he couldn't find a spot in the sand to his liking. He squirmed a good deal. Now and then his backside rose and fell. Cliff took one end of the blanket and Vernon the other, and they managed to hold it against the wind, flatten it to the sand. Charlene plopped down on it to keep it from blowing. It seemed only yesterday that Cliff and his father would put her in a blanket and toss her like a pillow, scaring her mother to death. Charlene was one of those girls who was more like a boy in the way nothing fazed her. Out of the water, toward Vernon, a girl came running so wet and glistening she looked naked.

"Look at that!" said Cliff, and then stood there, his mouth open, looking. She was actually naked. She ran right up and passed him, her feet kicking wet sand on him, then she dropped to lie for a moment on her face, then roll on her back. Only the gold-flecked sand clung to her white belly and breasts. Grains of sand, cinnamon colored, clung to her prominent, erectile nipples. Her eyes were closed, her head tipped to the left to avoid the wind. For a long moment Cliff gazed at her body as if in thought. When he blinked his eyes the peculiar thing was that he was the one who felt in the fishbowl. Surrounded by them. What did they think of a man down at the beach with all his clothes on? He was distracted by a tug on the blanket and turned to see Vernon pointing at the women. They waddled along like turtles. All he could wonder was what had ever led them to come to a beach. Buttoned at the collar, Janice's coat draped about her like a tent she was dragging. Cliff just stood there till they came along beside him, and May put out a hand to lean on him. Sand powdered her face.

"It's always so windy?" she asked Vernon.

"You folks call this windy?" May looked closely at him to see if he meant to be taken seriously. He surely knew, if he knew anything, that she knew more about wind than he did.

"Get Cliff to tell you how it blows around Chadron," she said. "It blows the words right out of your mouth, if you'd let it." Cliff was silent, so she added, "Don't it, Cliff?"

"Don't it what?" he answered. He allowed himself to turn so that his eyes went to the humped, squirming figure, under the blanket. The humping had pulled it up so the feet were uncovered. Four of them. Two of them were toes down, with tar spots on the bottoms: two of them were toes up, the heels dipped into the sand. In a story Cliff had heard but never fully understood, the point had hinged on the four-footed monster. Now he got the point.

"Blow the words right out of your mouth if you'd let it," said May. At a loss for words, Cliff moved to stand so he blocked her view. He took a grip on her hands and let her sag, puffing sour air at him, down to the blanket. "It's hard enough work just to get here," she said, and raised her eyes to squint at the water. "Charlene, you wanted to see the ocean: well, there it is."

Cliff was thinking that Charlene looked no older than the summer she was married. It was hard to understand her. She had had three children without ever growing up.

"If I'd known the sand was going to blow," said May, "we'd have stayed home to eat, then come over later. I hate sand in my food. Charlene, you going to sit down?"

Charlene stood there staring at a girl up to her ankles in the shallow water. She stooped to hold a child pressed to her front, the knees buckled up as if she squeezed it. A stream of water arched from the slit between the child's legs. The way she held it, pressed to her front, it was like squeezing juice from a bladder. There was nothing Cliff could do but wait for it to stop. Charlene's handbag dangled to where it almost dragged in the sand.

"That's Farrallon Island," said Vernon, pointing. Without his glasses Cliff couldn't see it. Janice tipped forward, as far as she could, to cup handfuls of sand over her ankles: she couldn't reach her feet. "We hear and read so much about their being so dirty," said May.

"It's the hippies," said Vernon. "They've taken it over."

Why was he such a fool as to say so? Even Cliff, who knew what he would see, twisted his head on his neck and looked all around him. The stark-naked girl had dried a lighter color: she didn't look so good. The sand sprinkled her like brown sugar, but the mole-colored nipples were flat on her breasts, like they'd been snipped off. At her feet, using her legs as a backrest, a lank-haired boy, chewing bubble gum, sunned his pimpled face. On his hairless chest someone had painted his nipples to look like staring eyes. Now that Cliff was seated it was plainer than ever what was going on under the blanket: the heels of two of the feet thrust deep into the sand, piling it up. Cliff felt the eyes of Janice on the back of his head, but he missed those of her mother. Where were they?

"Cliff," she said.

He did not turn to look.

"Cliff," she repeated.

At the edge of the water a dappled horse galloped with two long-haired, naked riders. If one was a boy, Cliff couldn't tell which was which.

"Who's ready for a beer?" asked Vernon, and peeled the towel off the basket. When no one replied he said, "Mr. Dickey, have yourself a beer," and took one. He moved the basket of food to where both Cliff and the women could reach it. Along with the bowl of potato salad there were two broiled chickens from the super-market. The chickens were still warm.

"All I've done since we left home is eat," Cliff said.

"We just ate," said Janice.

"We didn't drag all this stuff here," said Cliff, "just to turn around and drag it back." He took out the bowl of salad. He fished around in the basket for the paper cups and plates. He didn't look up at May until he knew for certain she had got her head and eyes around to the front. The sun glinted on her glasses. Absent-mindedly she raked her fingers across her forehead for loose strands of hair. "We eat the salad first or along with the chicken?"

None of the women made any comment. One of the maverick beach dogs, his coat heavy with sand, stood off a few yards and sniffed at the chicken. "They shouldn't allow dogs on a beach," said Cliff. "They run around and get hot and can't drink the water. In the heat they go mad."

"There's salt in there somewhere," said Janice. "I don't put all the salt I could on the salad."

Cliff took out one of the chickens, and using his fingers pried the legs off the body. He then broke the drumsticks off at the thighs, and placed the pieces on one of the plates.

"You still like the dark meat?" he said to Charlene. She

nodded her head. He peeled the plastic cover off the potato salad and forked it out on the paper plates. "Eat it before the sand gets at it," he said, and passed a plate to May. Janice reached to take one, and placed it on the slope of her lap. Vernon took the body of one of the birds, tore off the wings, and tossed one to the dog.

"I can't stand to see a dog watch me eat," he said.

"Vernon was in Korea for a year," said Janice.

Cliff began to eat. After the first few swallows it tasted all right. He hadn't been hungry at all when he started, but now he ate like he was famished. When he traveled all he seemed to do was sit and eat. He glanced up to see that they were all eating except for May, who just sat there. She had her head cocked sidewise as if straining to hear something. Not twenty yards away a boy plucked a guitar but Cliff didn't hear a sound with the wind against him. Two other boys, with shorts on, one with a top on, lay out on their bellies with their chins on their hands. One used a small rock to drive a short piece of wood into the sand. It was the idle sort of play Cliff would expect from a kid about six, not one about twenty. On the sand before them a shadow flashed and eight or ten feet away a bird landed, flapping its wings. Cliff had never set eyes on a bigger crow. He was shorter in the leg but as big as the gulls that strutted on the firm sand near the water. A little shabby at the tail, big glassy hatpin eyes. Cliff watched him dip his beak into the sand like one of these glass birds that go on drinking water, rocking on the perch. One of the boys said, "Hey, you, bird, come here!" and wiggled a finger at him. When the bird did just that Cliff couldn't believe his eyes. He had a stiff sort of strut, pumping his head, and favored one leg more than the other. No more than two feet away from the heads of those boys he stopped and gave them

17

a look. Either one of them might have reached out and touched him. Cliff had never seen a big, live bird as tame as that. The crows around Chadron were smarter than most people and had their own meetings and cawed crow language. They had discussions. You could hear them decide what to do next. The boy with the rock held it out toward him and damn if the crow didn't peck at it. Cliff could hear the click of his beak tapping the rock. He turned to see if May had caught that, but her eyes were on the plate in her lap.

"May, look—" he said.

Her eyes down she said, "I've seen all I want to see the rest of my life."

"The crow—" said Cliff, and took another look at him. He had his head cocked to one side, like a parrot, and his beak clamped down on one of the sticks driven into the sand. He tried to wiggle it loose as he tugged at it. He braced his legs and strained back like a robin pulling a worm from a hole. So Vernon wouldn't miss it, Cliff put out his hand to nudge him. "Well, I'll be damned," Vernon said.

Two little kids, one with a plastic pail, ran up to within about a yard of the bird, stopped and stared. He stared right back at them. Who was to say which of the two looked the strangest. The kids were naked as the day they were born. One was a boy. Whatever they had seen before they had never seen a crow that close up.

"Come on, bird," said the boy with the rock, and waved it. Nobody would ever believe it, but that bird took a tug at the stick, then rocked back and cawed. He made such a honk the kids were frightened. The little girl backed off and giggled. The crow clamped his beak on the stick again and had another try. A lanky-haired hippie girl, just out of the water, ran up and said, "Sam —are they teasing you, Sam?" She had on no top at all

18

but a pair of blue-jean shorts on her bottom. "Come on, bird!" yelled the boy with the rock, and pounded his fists on the sand. That crow had figured out a way to loosen up the stick by clamping down on it, hard, then moving in a circle, like he was drilling a well. He did that twice, then he pulled it free, clamped one claw on it, and cawed. "Good bird!" said the boy, and tried to take it from him, but that crow wouldn't let him. He backed off, flapped his wings, and soared off with his legs dangling. Cliff could see what it took a big bird like that to fly.

"What does he do with it?" said the girl. She looked off toward the cliffs where the bird had flown. Somewhere up there he had a lot of sticks: no doubt about that.

"Buries it," said the boy. "He thinks it's a bone."

The little girl with the plastic pail said, "Why don't you give him a real bone, then?" The boy and girl laughed. The hippie girl said, "Can I borrow a comb?" and the boy replied, "If you don't get sand in it." He moved so he could reach the comb in his pocket, and stroked it on his sleeve as he passed it to her. Combing her hair, her head tipped back, Cliff might have mistaken her for a boy. The little girl asked, "When will he do it again?"

"Soon as he's buried it," said the boy.

Cliff didn't believe that. He had watched crows all his life, but he had never seen a crow behave like that. He wanted to bring the point up, but how could he discuss it with a girl without her clothes on?

"Here he comes," said the boy, and there he was, his shadow flashing on the sand before them. He made a circle and came in for a landing on the firm sand. What if he did bury those sticks? His beak was shiny, yellow as a banana. "Come here, bird!" said the boy, and held out the rock, but the girl leaned forward and grabbed it from him.

19

"You want to hurt him?" she cried. "Why don't you give him a real bone?" She looked around as if she might see one, raking the sand with her hands.

"Here's one, miss!" said Cliff, and held the chicken leg out toward her. He could no more help himself than duck when someone took a swing at him. On her hands and knees the girl crawled toward him to where she could reach it. Her lank hair framed her face.

"There's meat on it," she said.

"Don't you worry," said Cliff, "crows like meat. They're really good meat-eaters."

She looked at him closely to see how he meant that. About her neck a fine gold-colored chain dangled an ornament. Cliff saw it plainly. Two brass nails were twisted to make some sort of puzzle. She looked at the bone Cliff had given her, the strip of meat on it, and turned to hold it out to the bird. He limped forward like he was trained and took it in his beak. Cliff caught his eye, and what worried him was that he might want to crow over it and drop it. He didn't want him to drop it and have to gulp down sandy meat. But that bird actually knew he had something unusual since he didn't put it down to clamp his claws on it. Instead he strutted. Up and down he went, like a sailor with a limp. Vernon laughed so hard he gave Cliff a slap on the knee. "Don't laugh at him," said the girl, and when she put out her hand he limped toward her to where she could touch him, stroking with her fingers the flat top of his head. The little boy suddenly yelled and ran around them in a circle, kicking up sand, and hooting. The crow took off. The heavy flap of his wings actually stirred the hair of the boy who was lying there, nearest to him; he raised one of his hands to wave as the bird soared away.

"I never seen anything like it!" said Vernon.

"Maybe you'd like to come oftener." Janice picked at the bread crumbs in her lap.

"Did you see him?" asked Cliff. "You get to see him?"

"We can go now if you men have eaten." May made a wad of the napkin and scraps in her lap, put them under the towel and plates in the basket.

Vernon said, "Honey, you see that crazy bird?"

Janice shaded her eyes with one hand, peered at the sky. Up there, high, a bird was wheeling. Cliff took it for a gull. The wind had caked the color she had put on her lips, and sand powdered the wrinkles around her eyes. Cliff remembered they were called crow's feet, which was how they looked. Now she lowered her hand and held it out to Vernon to pull her up. The sand caught up in the folds of her dress blew over May and the girl lying behind her, one arm across her face.

"People must be crazy to come and eat on a beach," said May.

Cliff pushed himself to his feet, sand clinging to his chicken-sticky fingers. He helped Vernon with the blanket, walking toward the water where they could shake it and not disturb people. A bearded youth without pants, but with a striped T-shirt, sat with crossed legs at the edge of the water. The horse that had galloped off to the south came galloping back with just one rider on it. Cliff could see it was a girl. Janice and her mother had begun the long walk back toward the car. Along the way they passed the naked girl, still sprawled on her back.

"She's going to get herself a sunburn," said Vernon.

To Charlene Cliff said, "You see that bird?" Charlene nodded. "Just remember you did, when I ask you. Nobody back in Chadron is going to believe me if you don't."

"What bird was it?" asked May.

21

"A crow," said Cliff.

"I would think you'd seen enough of crows," said May.

At the car Cliff turned for a last look at the beach. The tide had washed up a sort of reef so that he could no longer see the water. The girl and the dogs that ran along it were like black paper cutouts. Nobody would know if she had her clothes on or off. He had forgotten to check on the two of them who had been squirming under the blanket. One still lay there. The other one crouched with lowered head, as if reading something. From the back Cliff wouldn't know which one was the girl.

May said, "I've never before really believed it when I said that I can't believe my eyes, but now I believe it."

"You wouldn't believe them if you'd seen that crow," said Cliff.

"I didn't come all this way to look at a crow," she replied.

They all got into the car, and Cliff put the picnic basket into the rear. He took a moment, squinting, to see if the crazy bird had come back for more bones. If he had just thought, he would have given the girl the other two legs to feed him.

"I'd like a cup of coffee," said May, "but I'm willing to wait till we get home for it."

Vernon said, "Mr. Chalmers, you like me to drive?" Cliff agreed that he would. They went out through the gate where they had entered but the boy and the girl had left the booth. The chain was already half-covered with drifting sand.

"It's typical of your father," said May, "to drive all the way out here and look at a crow."

Charlene said, "Wait until I tell Leonard!" They looked to see what she would tell him. On the dry slope below them a small herd of cattle were being fed from a hovering helicopter. Bundles of straw were dropped to spread on the slope.

"If I were you," said May, "I'd tell him about *that* and nothing else."

Cliff felt his head wagging. He stopped it and said, "Charlene, now you tell him about that crow. What's a few crazy people to one crow in a million?"

There was no comment.

"We're going up now," said Vernon. "You feel that poppin' in your ears?"

1969

The Ram in the Thicket

In this dream Mr. Ormsby stood in the yard—at the edge of the yard where the weeds began—and stared at a figure that appeared to be on a rise. This figure had the head of a bird with a crown of bright, exotic plumage, only partially concealed by a paint-daubed helmet. Mr. Ormsby felt the urgent need to identify this strange bird. Feathery wisps of plumage shot through the crown of the helmet like a pillow leaking sharp spears of yellow straw. The face beneath it was indescribably solemn, with eyes so pale they were like openings on the sky. Slung over the left arm, casually, was a gun, but the right arm, the palm upward, extended toward a cloud of hovering birds. They came and went, like bees after honey, and there were so many and all so friendly, that Mr. Ormsby extended his own hand toward them. No birds came, but in his upturned palm he felt the dull throb of the alarm clock, which he held tenderly, a living thing, until it ran down.

In the morning light the photograph at the foot of his bed seemed startling. The boy stood alone on a rise, and he held, very casually, a gun. The face beneath the helmet had no features, but Mr. Ormsby would have known him just by the stance, by the way he held the gun. He held the gun like some women held their arms when their hands were idle, like parts of their body that for the moment were not much use. Without the gun it was as if some part of the boy had been amputated; the way he stood, even the way he walked was not quite right.

He had given the boy a gun because he had never had a gun himself and not because he wanted him to kill anything. The boy didn't want to kill anything either—he couldn't very well with his first gun because of the awful racket the beebees made in the barrel. He had given him a thousand-shot gun—but the rattle the beebees made in the barrel made it impossible for the boy to get close to anything. And *that* was what had made a hunter out of him. He had to stalk everything in order to get close enough to hit it, and after you stalk it you naturally want to hit something. When he got a gun that would really shoot, and only made a racket after he shot it, it was only natural that he shot it better than anyone else. He said shoot, because the boy never seemed to realize that when he shot and hit something, the something was dead. He simply didn't realize this side of things at all. But when he brought a rabbit home and fried it—by himself, for Mother wouldn't let *him* touch

it—he never kidded them about the meat they ate themselves. He never really knew whether the boy did that
out of kindness for Mother, or simply because he never
thought about such things. He never seemed to feel like
talking much about anything. He would sit and listen to
Mother—he had never once been disrespectful—nor had
he ever once heeded anything she said. He would listen,
respectfully, and that was all. It was a known fact that
Mother knew more about birds and bird migration than
anyone in the state of Pennsylvania—except the boy. It
was clear to him that the boy knew more, but for years
it had been Mother's business and it meant more to her
—the business did—than to the boy. But it was only
natural that a woman who founded the League for Wild
Life Conservation would be upset by a boy who lived
with a gun. It was only natural—he was upset himself by
the *idea* of it—but the boy and his gun somehow never
bothered him. He had never seen a boy and a dog, or a
boy and anything, any closer—and if the truth were
known both the boy's dogs knew it, nearly died of it. Not
that he wasn't friendly, or as nice to them as any boy, but
they knew they simply didn't rate in a class with his gun.
Without that gun the boy himself really looked funny,
didn't know how to stand, and nearly fell over if you
talked to him. It was only natural that he enlisted, and
there was nothing he ever heard that surprised him less
than the making a hero out of him. Nothing more natural than that they should name something after him. If
the boy had had his choice it would have been a gun
rather than a boat, a thousand-shot, non-rattle BB gun
named Ormsby. But it would kill Mother if she knew—
maybe it would kill nearly anybody—what he thought
was the most natural thing of all. Let God strike him
dead if he had known anything righter, anything more
natural, than that the boy should be killed. That was

26

something he could not explain, and would certainly never mention to Mother unless he slipped up some night and talked in his sleep.

He turned slowly on the bed, careful to keep the springs quiet, and as he lowered his feet he scooped his socks from the floor. As a precaution Mother had slept the first few months of their marriage in her corset—as a precaution and as an aid to self-control. In the fall they had ordered twin beds. Carrying his shoes—today, of all days, would be a trial for Mother—he tiptoed to the closet and picked up his shirt and pants. There was simply no reason, as he had explained to her twenty years ago, why she should get up when he could just as well get a bite for himself. He had made that suggestion when the boy was just a baby and she needed her strength. Even as it was she didn't come out of it any too well. The truth was, Mother was so thorough about everything she did that her breakfasts usually took an hour or more. When he did it himself he was out of the kitchen in ten, twelve minutes and without leaving any pile of dishes around. By himself he could quick-rinse them in a little hot water, but with Mother there was the dish pan and all of the suds. Mother had the idea that a meal simply wasn't a meal without setting the table and using half the dishes in the place. It was easier to do it himself, and except for Sunday, when they had brunch, he was out of the house an hour before she got up. He had a bite of lunch at the store and at four o'clock he did the day's shopping since he was right downtown anyway. There was a time he called her up and inquired as to what she thought she wanted, but since he did all the buying he knew that better himself. As secretary for the League of Women Voters she had enough on her mind in times like these without cluttering it up with food. Now that he left the store an hour early he usually got home in the

27

midst of her nap or while she was taking her bath. As he had nothing else to do he prepared the vegetables, and dressed the meat, as Mother had never shown much of a flair for meat. There had been a year—when the boy was small and before he had taken up that gun—when she had made several marvelous lemon meringue pies. But feeling as she did about the gun—and she told them both how she felt about it—she didn't see why she should slave in the kitchen for people like that. She always spoke to them as *they*—or as *you* plural—from the time he had given the boy the gun. Whether this was because they were both men, both culprits, or both something else, they were never entirely separate things again. When she called, *they* would both answer, and though the boy had been gone two years he still felt him *there*, right beside him, when Mother said *you*.

For some reason he could not understand—although the rest of the house was neat as a pin, too neat—the room they *lived* in was always a mess. Mother refused to let the cleaning woman set her foot in it. Whenever she left the house she locked the door. Long, long ago he had said something, and she had said something, and she had said she had wanted one room in the house where she could relax and just let her hair down. That had sounded so wonderfully human, so unusual for Mother, that he had been completely taken with it. As a matter of fact he still didn't know what to say. It was the only room in the house—except for the screened-in porch in the summer —where he could take off his shoes and open his shirt on his underwear. If the room was *clean*, it would be clean like all of the others, and that would leave him nothing but the basement and the porch. The way the boy took to the out-of-doors—he stopped looking for his cuff links, began to look for pins—was partially because he couldn't find a place in the house to sit down. They had just redecorated the house—the boy at that time was just a little shaver—and Mother had spread newspapers over everything. There hadn't been a chair in the place—except the straight-backed ones at the table—that hadn't been, that *wasn't* covered with a piece of newspaper. Anyone who had ever scrunched around on a paper knew what that was like. It was at that time that he had got the idea of having his pipe in the basement, reading in the bedroom, and the boy had taken to the out-of-doors. Because he had always wanted a gun himself, and because the boy was alone, with no kids around to play with, he had brought him home that damn gun. A thousand-shot gun by the name of Daisy—funny that he should remember the name—and five thousand beebees in a drawstring canvas bag.

That gun had been a mistake—he began to shave himself in tepid, lukewarm water rather than let it run hot, which would bang the pipes and wake Mother up. That gun had been a mistake—when the telegram came that the boy had been killed Mother hadn't said a word, but she made it clear whose fault it was. There was never any doubt, *any* doubt, as to just whose fault it was.

He stopped thinking while he shaved, attentive to the mole at the edge of his mustache, and leaned to the mirror to avoid dropping suds on the rug. There had been a time when he had wondered about an Oriental throw-rug in the bathroom, but over twenty years he had become accustomed to it. As a matter of fact he sort of missed it whenever they had guests with children and Mother remembered to take it up. Without the rug he always felt just a little uneasy, a little naked, in the bathroom, and this made him whistle or turn on the water and let it run. If it hadn't been for that he might not have noticed as soon as he did that Mother did the same thing whenever anybody was in the house. She turned on the water and let it run until she was through with the toilet, then she would flush it before she turned the water off. If you happen to have old-fashioned plumbing, and have lived with a person for twenty years, you can't help noticing little things like that. He had got to be a little like that himself: since the boy had gone he used the one in the basement or waited until he got down to the store. As a matter of fact it was more convenient, didn't wake Mother up, and he could have his pipe while he was sitting there.

With his pants on, but carrying his shirt—for he might get it soiled preparing breakfast—he left the bathroom and tiptoed down the stairs.

Although the boy had gone, was gone, that is, Mother still liked to preserve her slipcovers and the kitchen linoleum. It was a good piece, well worth preserving, but unless there were guests in the house he never saw it— he nearly forgot that it was there. The truth was he had to look at it once a week, every time he put down the papers—but right now he couldn't tell you what color that linoleum was! He couldn't do it, and wondering what in the world color it was he bent over and peeked at it—blue. Blue and white, Mother's favorite colors of course.

Suddenly he felt the stirring in his bowels. Usually this occurred while he was rinsing the dishes after his second cup of coffee or after the first long draw on his pipe. He was not supposed to smoke in the morning, but it was more important to be regular that way than irregular with his pipe. Mother had been the first to realize this—not in so many words—but she would rather he did anything than not be able to do *that*.

He measured out a pint and a half of water, put it over a medium fire, and added just a pinch of salt. Then he walked to the top of the basement stairs, turned on the light, and at the bottom turned it off. He dipped his head to pass beneath a sagging line of wash, the sleeves dripping, and with his hands out, for the corner was dark, he entered the cell.

The basement toilet had been put in to accommodate the help, who had to use something, and Mother would not have them on her Oriental rug. Until the day he dropped some money out of his pants and had to strike a match to look for it, he had never noticed what kind of a stool it was. Mother had picked it up secondhand—she had never told him where—because she couldn't see buying something new for a place always in the dark. It was very old, with a chain pull, and operated on a principle that invariably produced quite a splash. But in spite of that, he preferred it to the one at the store and very much more than the one upstairs. This was rather hard to explain since the seat was pretty cold in the winter and the water sometimes nearly froze. But it was private like no other room in the house. Considering that the house was as good as empty, that was a strange thing to say, but it was the only way to say how he felt. If he went off for a walk like the boy, Mother would miss him, somebody would see him, and he wouldn't feel right about it anyhow. All he wanted was a dark, quiet place and the feeling that for five minutes, just five minutes, nobody would be looking for him. Who would ever believe five minutes like that were so hard to come by? The closest he had ever been to the boy—after he had given him the gun—was the morning he had found him here on the stool. It was then that the boy had said, *et tu, Brutus,* and they had both laughed so hard they had had to hold their sides. The boy had put his head in a basket of wash so Mother wouldn't hear. Like everything the boy said there were two or three ways to take it, and in the dark Mr. Ormsby could not see his face. When he stopped

31

laughing the boy said, *Well, Pop, I suppose one flush ought to do,* but Mr. Ormsby had not been able to say anything. To be called Pop made him so weak that he had to sit right down on the stool, just like he was, and support his head in his hands. Just as he had never had a name for the boy, the boy had never had a name for him—none, that is, that Mother would permit him to use. Of all the names Mother couldn't stand, Pop was the worst, and he agreed with her, it was vulgar, common, and used by strangers to intimidate old men. He agreed with her, completely—until he heard the word in the boy's mouth. It was only natural that the boy would use it if he ever had the chance—but he never dreamed that any word, especially *that* word, could mean what it did. It made him weak, he had to sit down and pretend he was going about his business, and what a blessing it was that the place was dark. Nothing more was said, ever, but it remained their most important conversation—so important they were afraid to try and improve on it. Days later he remembered the rest of the boy's sentence, and how shocking it was but without any *sense* of shock. A blow so sharp that he had no sense of pain, only a knowing, as he had under gas, that he had been worked on. For two, maybe three minutes, there in the dark they had been what Mother called them, they were *they*— and they were there in the basement because they were so much alike. When the telegram came, and when he knew what he would find, he had brought it there, had struck a match, and read what it said. The match filled the cell with light and he saw—he couldn't help seeing—piles of tinned goods in the space beneath the stairs. Several dozen cans of tuna fish and salmon, and since *he* was the one that had the points, bought the groceries, there was only one place Mother could have got such things. It had been a greater shock than the telegram—that was the honest-to-God's truth and anyone who knew Mother as well as he did would have felt the same. It was unthinkable, but there it was—and there were more on top of the water closet, where he peered while precariously balanced on the stool. Cans of pineapple, crabmeat, and tins of Argentine beef. He had been stunned, the match had burned down and actually scorched his fingers, and he nearly killed himself when he forgot and stepped off the seat. Only later in the morning—after he had sent flowers to ease the blow for Mother—did he realize how such a thing *must* have occurred. Mother knew so many influential people, and before the war they gave her so much, that they had very likely given her all of this stuff as well. Rather than turn it down and needlessly alienate people, influential people, Mother had done the next best thing. While the war was on she refused to serve it, or profiteer in any way—and at the same time not alienate people foolishly. It had been an odd thing, certainly, that he should discover all of that by the same match that he read the telegram. Naturally, he never breathed a word of it to Mother, as something like that, even though she was not superstitious, would really upset her. It was one of those things that he and the boy would keep to themselves.

It would be like Mother to think of putting it in here, the very last place that the cleaning woman would look for it. The new cleaning woman would neither go upstairs nor down, and did whatever she did somewhere else. Mr. Ormsby lit a match to see if everything was all right—hastily blew it out when he saw that the can pile had increased. He stood up—then hurried up the stairs without buttoning his pants as he could hear the water boiling. He added half a cup, then measured three heaping tablespoons of coffee into the bottom of the double boiler, buttoned his pants. Looking at his watch he saw

that it was seven thirty-five. As it would be a hard day
—sponsoring a boat was a man-size job—he would give
Mother another ten minutes or so. He took two bowls
from the cupboard, sat them on blue pottery saucers, and
with the grapefruit knife in his hand walked to the icebox.

As he put his head in the icebox door—in order to see
he had to—Mr. Ormsby stopped breathing and closed
his eyes. What had been dying for some time was now
dead. He leaned back, inhaled, leaned in again. The floor
of the icebox was covered with a fine assortment of jars
full of leftovers Mother simply could not throw away.
Some of the jars were covered with little oilskin hoods,
some with saucers, and some with paper snapped on
with a rubber band. It was impossible to tell, from the
outside, which one it was. Seating himself on the floor he
removed them one at a time, starting at the front and
working toward the back. As he had done this many
times before, he got well into the problem, near the
middle, before troubling to sniff anything. A jar that
might have been carrots—it was hard to tell without
probing—was now a furry marvel of green mold. It
smelled only mildly, however, and Mr. Ormsby remembered that this was penicillin, the life-giver. A spoonful
of cabbage—it had been three months since they had had
cabbage—had a powerful stench but was still not the one
he had in mind. There were two more jars of mold, the
one screwed tight he left alone as it had a frosted look
and the top of the lid bulged. The culprit, however, was
not that at all, but in an open saucer on the next shelf—
part of an egg—Mr. Ormsby had beaten the white himself. He placed the saucer on the sink and returned all
but two of the jars to the icebox: the cabbage and the
explosive looking one. If it smelled he took it out, otherwise Mother had to see for herself as she refused to take

34

their word for these things. When he was just a little shaver the boy had walked into the living room full of Mother's guests and showed them something in a jar. Mother had been horrified—but she naturally thought it a frog or something and not a bottle out of her own icebox. When one of the ladies asked the boy where in the world he had found it, he naturally said, *In the icebox.* Mother had never forgiven him. After that she forbade him to look in the box without permission, and the boy had not so much as peeked in it since. He would eat only what he found on the table, or ready to eat in the kitchen —or what he found at the end of those walks he took everywhere.

With the jar of cabbage and furry mold Mr. Ormsby made a trip to the garage, picked up the garden spade, walked around behind. At one time he had emptied the jars and merely buried the contents, but recently, since the war that is, he had buried it all. Part of it was a question of time—he had more work to do at the store —but the bigger part of it was to put an end to the jars. Not that it worked out that way—all Mother had to do was open a new one—but it gave him a real satisfaction to bury them. Now that the boy and his dogs were gone there was simply no one around the house to eat up all the food Mother saved.

There were worms in the fork of earth he had turned and he stood looking at them—*they* both had loved worms—when he remembered the water boiling on the stove. He dropped everything and ran, ran right into Emil Ludlow, the milkman, before he noticed him. Still on the run he went up the steps and through the screen door into the kitchen—he was clear to the stove before he remembered the door would slam. He started back, but too late, and in the silence that followed the BANG he stood with his eyes tightly closed, his fists clenched.

Usually he remained in this condition until a sign from Mother—a thump on the floor or her voice at the top of the stairs. None came, however, only the sound of the milk bottles that Emil Ludlow was leaving on the porch. Mr. Ormsby gave him time to get away, waited until he heard the horse walking, then he went out and brought the milk in. At the icebox he remembered the water— why it was he had come running in the first place—and he left the door open and hurried to the stove. It was down to half a cup but not, thank heavens, dry. He added a full pint, then returned and put the milk in the icebox; took out the butter, four eggs, and a Flori-gold grapefruit. Before he cut the grapefruit he looked at his watch and seeing that it was ten minutes to eight, an hour before train time, he opened the stairway door.

"Ohhh, Mother!" he called, and then he returned to the grapefruit.

Ad astra per aspera, she said, and rose from the bed. In the darkness she felt about for her corset, then let herself go completely for the thirty-five seconds it required to get it on. This done, she pulled the cord to the light that hung in the attic, and as it snapped on, in a firm voice she said, *Fiat lux*. Light having been made, Mother opened her eyes.

As the bulb hung in the attic, thirty feet away and out of sight, the closet remained in an afterglow, a twilight zone. It was not light, strictly speaking, but it was all Mother wanted to see. Seated on the attic stairs she trimmed her toenails with a pearl-handled knife that Mr. Ormsby had been missing for several years. The blade was not so good any longer and using it too freely had resulted in ingrown nails on both of her big toes. But Mother preferred it to scissors which were proven, along with bathtubs, to be one of the most dangerous things in

36

the home. *Even more than the battlefield, the most dangerous place in the world. Dry feet and hands before turning on lights, dry between toes.*

Without stooping she slipped into her sabots and left the closet, the light burning, and with her eyes dimmed, but not closed, went down the hall. Locking the bathroom door she stepped to the basin and turned on the cold water, then she removed several feet of paper from the toilet-paper roll. This took time, as in order to keep the roller from squeaking, it had to be removed from its socket in the wall, then returned. One piece she put in the pocket of her kimono, the other she folded into a wad and used as a blotter to dab up spots on the floor. Turning up the water she sat down on the stool—then she got up to get a pencil and pad from the table near the window. On the first sheet she wrote—

> *Ars longa, vita brevis*
> Wildflower club, sun. 4 p.m.

She tore this off and filed it, tip showing, right at the front of her corset. On the next page—

> ROGER—
> Ivory Snow
> Sani-Flush on thurs.

As she placed this on top of the toilet paper roll she heard him call "First for breakfast." She waited until he closed the stairway door, then she stood up and turned on the shower. As it rained into the tub and splashed behind her in the basin, she lowered the lid, flushed the toilet. Until the water closet had filled, stopped gurgling, she stood at the window watching a squirrel cross the yard from tree to tree. Then she turned the shower off and noisily dragged the shower curtain, on its metal rings, back to the wall. She dampened her shower cap in the basin and

37

hung it on the towel rack to dry, dropping the towel that was there down the laundry chute. This done, she returned to the basin and held her hands under the running water, now cold, until she was awake. With her index finger she massaged her gums—*there is no pyorrhea among the Indians*—and then, with the tips of her fingers, she dampened her eyes.

She drew the blind, and in the half-light the room seemed to be full of lukewarm water, greenish in color. With a piece of Kleenex, she dried her eyes, then turned it to gently blow her nose, first the left side, then with a little more blow on the right. There was nothing to speak of, nothing, so she folded the tissue, slipped it into her pocket. Raising the blind, she faced the morning with her eyes softly closed, letting the light come in as prescribed—gradually. Eyes wide, she then stared for a full minute at the yard full of grackles, covered with grackles, before she actually saw them. Running to the door, her head in the hall, her arm in the bathroom wildly pointing, she tried to whisper, loud-whisper to him, but her voice cracked.

"Roger," she called, a little hoarsely. "The window—run!"

She heard him turn from the stove and skid on the newspapers, bump into the sink, curse, then get up and on again.

"Blackbirds?" he whispered.

"Grackles!" she said, for the thousandth time she said *Grackles.*

"They're pretty!" he said.

"Family—" she said, ignoring him, "family *Icteridae* American."

"Well—" he said.

"Roger!" she said; "something's burning."

She heard him leave the window and on his way back

38

to the stove, on the same turn, skid on the papers again. She left him there and went down the hall to the bedroom, closed the door, and passed between the mirrors once more to the closet. From five dresses—*any woman with more than five dresses, at this time, should have the vote taken away from her*—she selected the navy blue sheer with pink lace yoke and kerchief, short bolero. At the back of the closet—but in order to see she had to return to the bathroom, look for the flashlight in the drawer full of rags and old tins of shoe polish—were three shelves, each supporting ten to twelve pairs of shoes, and a large selection of slippers were piled on the floor. On the second shelf were the navy blue pumps—*we all have one weakness, but between men and shoes you can give me shoes*—navy blue pumps with a Cuban heel and a small bow. She hung the dress from the neck of the floor lamp, placed the shoes on the bed. From beneath the bed she pulled a hat box—the hat was new. Navy straw with shasta daisies, pink geraniums and a navy blue veil with pink and white fuzzy dots. She held it out where it could be seen in the mirror, front and side, without seeing herself —*it's not every day that one sponsors a boat.* Not every day, and she turned to the calendar on her night table, a bird calendar featuring the natural-color male goldfinch for the month of June. Under the date of June 23 she printed the words, FAMILY ICTERIDAE—YARDFUL, and beneath it—

Met Captain Sudcliffe and gave him U.S.S. *Ormsby*

When he heard Mother's feet on the stairs Mr. Ormsby cracked her soft-boiled eggs and spooned them carefully into her heated cup. He had spilled his own on the floor when he had run to look at the black—or whatever color they were—birds. As they were very, very soft he had merely wiped them up. As he buttered the toast —the four burned slices were on the back porch airing

—Mother entered the kitchen and said, "Roger—*more* toast?"

"I was watching blackbirds," he said.

"Grack-les," she said, "Any bird is a *black*bird if the males are largely or entirely black."

Talk about male and female birds really bothered Mr. Ormsby. Although she was a girl of the old school Mother never hesitated, *anywhere*, to speak right out about male and female birds. A cow was a cow, a bull was a bull, but to Mr. Ormsby a bird was a bird.

"Among the birdfolk," said Mother, "the menfolk, so to speak, wear the feathers. The female has more serious work to do."

"How does that fit the blackbirds?" said Mr. Ormsby.

"Every rule," said Mother, "has an exception."

There was no denying the fact that the older Mother got the more distinguished she appeared. As for himself, what he saw in the mirror looked very much like the Roger Ormsby that had married Violet Ames twenty years ago. As the top of his head got hard the bottom tended to get a little soft, but otherwise there wasn't much change. But it was hard to believe that Mother was the pretty little pop-eyed girl—he had thought it was her corset that popped them—whose nipples had been like buttons on her dress. Any other girl would have looked like a you-know—but there wasn't a man in Media County, or anywhere else, who ever mentioned it. A man could think what he would think, but he was the only man who really knew what Mother was like. And how little she was like *that*.

"Three-seven-four East one-one-six," said Mother.

That was the way her mind worked, all over the place on one cup of coffee—birds one moment, Mrs. Dinardo the next.

He got up from the table and went after Mrs. Dinardo's letter—Mother seldom had time to read them unless he read them to her. Returning, he divided the rest of the coffee between them, unequally: three-quarters for Mother, a swallow of grounds for himself. He waited a moment, wiping his glasses, while Mother looked through the window at another blackbird. "Cowbird," she said, *"Molothrus ater."*

" 'Dear Mrs. Ormsby,' " Mr. Ormsby began. Then he stopped to scan the page, as Mrs. Dinardo had a strange style and was not much given to writing letters. " 'Dear Mrs. Ormsby,' " he repeated, " 'I received your letter and I Sure was glad to know that you are both well and I know you often think of me I often think of you too—' " He paused to get his breath—Mrs. Dinardo's style was not much for pauses—and to look at Mother. But Mother was still with the cowbird. " 'Well, Mrs. Ormsby,' " he continued, " 'I haven't a thing in a room that I know of the people that will be away from the room will be only a week next month. But come to See me I may have Something if you don't get Something.' " Mrs. Dinardo, for some reason, always capitalized the letter S which along with everything else didn't make it easier to read. " 'We are both well and he is Still in the Navy Yard. My I do wish the war was over it is So long. We are So tired of it do come and See us when you give them your boat. Wouldn't a Street be better than a boat? If you are going to name Something why not a Street? Here in my hand is news of a boat Sunk what is wrong with Ormsby on a Street? Well 116 is about the Same we have the river and its nice. If you don't find Something See me I may have Something. Best Love, Mrs. Myrtle Dinardo.' "

It was quite a letter to get from a woman that Mother had known, known Mother, that is, for nearly eighteen years. Brought in to nurse the boy—he could never un-

derstand why a woman like Mother, with her figure—
but anyhow, Mrs. Dinardo was brought in. Something
in her milk, Dr. Paige said, when it was as plain as the
nose on your face it was nothing in the milk, but something in the boy. He just refused, plain refused, to nurse
with Mother. The way the little rascal would look at her,
but not a sound out of him but gurgling when Mrs.
Dinardo would scoop him up and go upstairs to their
room—the only woman—other woman, that is, that
Mother ever let step inside of it. She had answered an ad
that Mother had run, on Dr. Paige's suggestion, and they
had been like *that* from the first time he saw them.

"I'll telephone," said Mother.

On the slightest provocation Mother would call Mrs.
Dinardo by long distance—she had to come down four
flights of stairs to answer—and tell her she was going to
broadcast over the radio or something. Although Mrs.
Dinardo hardly knew one kind of bird from another,
Mother sent her printed copies of every single one of her
bird-lore lectures. She also sent her hand-pressed flowers
from the garden.

"I'll telephone," repeated Mother.

"My own opinion—" began Mr. Ormsby, but stopped
when Mother picked up her eggcup, made a pile of her
plates, and started toward the sink. "I'll take care of
that," he said. "Now you run along and telephone." But
Mother walked right by him and took her stand at the
sink. With one hand—with the other she held her
kimono close about her—she let the water run into a
large dish pan. Mr. Ormsby had hoped to avoid this; now
he would have to first rinse, then dry, every piece of
silver and every dish they had used. As Mother could
only use one hand it would be even slower than usual.

"We don't want to miss our local," he said. "You better

run along and let me do it."

"Cold water," she said, "for the eggs." He had long ago learned not to argue with Mother about the fine points of washing pots, pans, or dishes with bits of egg. He stood at the sink with the towel while she went about trying to make suds with a piece of stale soap in a little wire cage. As Mother refused to use a fresh piece of soap, nothing remotely like suds ever appeared. For this purpose, he kept a box of Gold Dust Twins concealed beneath the sink, and when Mother turned her back he slipped some in.

"There now," Mother said, and placed the rest of the dishes in the water, rinsed her fingers under the tap, paused to sniff at them.

"My own opinion—" Mr. Ormsby began, but stopped when Mother raised her finger, the index finger with the scar from the wart she once had. They stood quiet, and Mr. Ormsby listened to the water drip in the sink—the night before he had come down in his bare feet to shut it off. All of the taps dripped now and there was just nothing to do about it but put a rag or something beneath it to break the ping.

"Thrush!" said Mother. "Next to the nightingale the most popular of European songbirds."

"Very pretty," he said, although he simply couldn't hear a thing. Mother walked to the window, folding the collar of her kimono over her bosom and drawing the tails into a hammock beneath her behind. Mr. Ormsby modestly turned away. He quick-dipped one hand into the Gold Dust—drawing it out as he slipped it into the dish pan and worked up a suds.

As he finished wiping the dishes she came in with a bouquet for Mrs. Dinardo and arranged it, for the moment, in a tall glass.

43

"According to her letter," Mrs. Ormsby said, "she isn't too sure of having something— Roger!" she said. "You're dripping."

Mr. Ormsby put his hands over the sink and said, "If we're going to be met right at the station I don't see where you're going to see Mrs. Dinardo. You're going to be met at the station and then you're going to sponsor the boat. My own opinion is that after the boat we come on home."

"I know that street of hers," said Mother. "There isn't a wildflower on it!"

On the wall above the icebox was a pad of paper and a blue pencil hanging by a string. As Mother started to write the point broke off, fell behind the icebox.

"Mother," he said, "you ever see my knife?"

"Milkman," said Mother. "If we're staying overnight we won't need milk in the morning."

In jovial tones Mr. Ormsby said, "I'll bet we're right back here before dark." That was all, that was ALL that he said. He had merely meant to call her attention to the fact that Mrs. Dinardo said—all but said—that she didn't have a room for them. But when Mother turned he saw that her mustache was showing, a sure sign that she was mad.

"Well—now," Mother said, and lifting the skirt of her kimono swished around the cabinet and then he heard her on the stairs. From the landing at the top of the stairs she said, "In that case I'm sure there's no need for *my* going. I'm sure the Navy would just as soon have you. After all," she said, "it's *your* name on the boat!"

"Now, Mother," he said, just as she closed the door, *not* slammed it, just closed it as quiet and nice as you'd please. Although he had been through this a thousand times it seemed he was never ready for it, never knew when it would happen, never felt anything but nearly sick. He went into the front room and sat down on the chair near the piano—then got up to arrange the doily at the back of his head. Ordinarily he could leave the house and after three or four days it would blow over, but in all his life—their life—there had been nothing like this. The government of the United States—he got up again and called, "OHHhhhh, Mother!"

No answer.

He could hear her moving around upstairs, but as she often went back to bed after a spat, just moving around didn't mean much of anything. He came back into the front room and sat down on the milk stool near the fireplace. It was the only seat in the room not protected with newspapers. The only thing the boy ever sat on when he had to sit on something. Somehow, thinking about that made him stand up. He could sit in the lawn swing, in the front yard, if Mother hadn't told everybody in town why it was that he, Roger Ormsby, would have to take the day off—not to sit in the lawn swing, not by a long shot. Everybody knew—Captain Sudcliffe's nice letter had appeared on the first page of the *Graphic*, under a picture of Mother leading a bird-lore hike in the Poconos. This picture bore the title LOCAL WOMAN HEADS DAWN BUSTERS, and marked Mother's appearance on the national bird-lore scene. But it was not one of her best pictures—it dated from way back in the twenties and those hipless dresses and round, bucket hats were not Mother's type. Until they saw that picture, and the letter beneath it, some people had forgotten that Virgil was missing, and most of them seemed to think it was a good idea to swap him for a boat. The U.S.S. *Ormsby* was a permanent sort of thing. Although he was born and raised in the town hardly anybody knew very much about Virgil, but they all were pretty familiar with his boat. "How's that boat of yours coming along?" they would say, but in more than twenty years nobody had ever asked him about *his* boy. Whose boy? Well, that was just the point. Everyone agreed Ormsby was a fine name for a boat.

It would be impossible to explain to Mother, maybe to anybody for that matter, what this U.S.S. *Ormsby* business meant to him. "The" boy and "the" *Ormsby*—it was a pretty strange thing that they both had the definite article, and gave him the feeling he was facing a monument.

"Oh Rog-gerrr!" Mother called.

"Coming," he said, and made for the stairs.

From the bedroom Mother said, "However I might feel personally, I do have my *own* name to think of. I am not one of these people who can do as they please— Roger, are you listening?"

"Yes, Mother," he said.

"—with their life."

As he went around the corner he found a note pinned to the door.

> Bathroom window up
> Cellar door down
> Is it blue or brown for Navy?

He stopped on the landing and looked up the stairs.

"Did you say something?" she said.

"No, Mother—" he said, then he added, "it's blue. For the Navy, Mother, it's blue."

1948

Here Is Einbaum

Here is Einbaum at an open casement window, three floors above the street. On the corner just below him, barefooted, a beggar stands in the fresh fall of snow. His head is bare. He has tipped his face so that Einbaum can see his beard. Before him, in an attitude of prayer, the palms of his hands are pressed together, with a narrow slit for coins between his thumbs. He sings. Someone from a window below Einbaum has tossed him a coin. It is searched for in the snow by two shabby children and the woman who holds a third child at her hip. The head and feet of this child are bare, but it looks well fed. Einbaum has been told that these cunning beggars rent the children from people who have too many, but the woman who told him this is the one who dropped the coin. What is he to believe—that she is wrong, or merely a fool? Until he was told, he sometimes dropped a coin himself. When the beggar sang Christmas carols, the children joined in, their mouths round and dark in their pale white faces. Einbaum's delight was in the sensation that they were needy and he could help them; his torment in the certain knowledge that he was a fool. In the room behind Einbaum the ceiling is high and his sister, Ilse, sits sewing on buttons. She is paid by the button. Her scalp gleams white at the part of her hair. Einbaum steps back from the window to let the housemaid, Karina, air out the bolster and puff the pillows, and they both stand waiting, knowing that the dust will make her sneeze.

Here is Einbaum in the woods of the Wienerwald, concealed by shadows and leaves. He lies sprawled on his face; we see only the soles of his boots and the rucksack strapped to his back. One arm is crooked beneath his head. The other grips an unloaded military rifle. Einbaum is in the midst of the training exercises he enjoys much more than he does his freedom. He is good at it. He can tramp with his pack eighteen miles a day. In his group it is openly admitted that if there is war Einbaum will rise fast. He likes to serve. He likes the simple, orderly life. On him and around him glows the golden light of a melancholy Viennese fall, the leaves crushed by lovers who have been careful to stub their cigarettes.

Here is Einbaum at the Studenten Klub, seated at the window overlooking the Schottengasse: snow is falling. It blurs the Christmas lights and the spire of Stefansdom. Einbaum strains to read the time on the glowing face of a clock. The woman seated at his side is his mistress, Frau Koenig. She wears galoshes that are wet and give off an odor. He is only at his ease with her, she tells him, when they are in bed. Little if anything ever said to Einbaum, up to this moment, has pleased him so much. Einbaum the heartless rogue. Einbaum the callous sensualist. It is unimportant, for the time being, that he is also not at ease with her in bed. Part of the problem is technical. He sometimes fears he might suffocate. Her gloved hands rest on her wide matron's lap. Frau Koenig hasn't given him much pleasure, but she has given Einbaum great plans. He will be a roué. Generous matrons will support him in the manner to which he will one day be accustomed. As the snow falls he wonders what time it is. Frau Koenig will misinterpret Einbaum's glancing at his watch, which happened to be the one she gave him. Now it is Christmas. Before buying her something he would like to know what she intends to give him.

We might doubt it, but this, too, is Einbaum. He wears a bowler and carries a valise. It is heavy with books necessary to his life at the University. Two volumes of Spengler, Count Keyserling's *Travel Diary*, one book of Italian grammar, another of Italian history. There is also a separate folder of notes, written in code. Einbaum the revolutionary, the *agent provocateur*, waits on the steps of the university for a colleague from Graz, Herr L—— (Einbaum will always see it with the letters missing) who, with Einbaum, will create the disturbance initiating the new order in Vienna. The password is *Oesterreich über alles*, unlikely as it seems. While running from this scene, which proved to be a fiasco, he is pursued by a man no longer than Dollfuss, who fires a shot that turns up in the second volume of Einbaum's Spengler—a lead pellet he later attached to the fob of his watch. He liked intrigue. He considered an offer that would set him up, comfortably, in Buda. It was one of his options when something more interesting intervened.

Once more, here is Einbaum—but does it matter? Ev-

49

eryone has an album full of such snapshots. Few, of course, were ever taken by the camera, but they remain indelible on the lens of the eye. In the dark, as a rule, one sees them the clearest, glowing like figures on the face of a watch. Why these and not others? Einbaum often wonders. Something to do with his own life and torment. He cannot spell it out, but in these recurring snapshots the film of his life had its reruns. He studied it for clues to what later happened: some inkling, some suggestion, of emerging powers. Nothing unusual. The same vague apprehensions common to millions of German Jews. Mendelssohn Einbaum often feared for his life, but that was hardly news.

With shame he admits it, but a German first. Both sides of the family burghers in Linz, where they specialized in leather tanning. Einbaum's Jewish grandfather used to say Austria is a condition from which Germans must recover. Perhaps Einbaum did not. He was born in Vienna—his mother, Elsa Nottebaum, an actress of some importance in Hofmannsthal's plays. Einbaum's grandmother wore the family jewels on a cord between her breasts, where they acquired a patina. Is it possible to be a German and a Jew? Einbaum stands before you. Other people's clothes fit him better than his own. The way he backs into a chair, or crooks his finger into the coin slot of a pay phone, the way he nods his head, like a finger, when speaking, or juts it forward, wagging, when listening, the way his coat gapes open like a tent flap—but the impression is clearer across the room than when face to face. A German, unmistakably, and more or less mistakably, a Jew. Was it the German or the Jew in him that seemed to be the clearest that day in August 1939? The century was ten years older than Einbaum. He walked in a drizzle on Kärntnerstrasse. Where the street bends and opens on Stefansdom he stepped from the curb to make way for two ladies. The hair of one was damp. His face actually brushed it as he dipped his head beneath her umbrella. It is why a moment passes before he notes the cab pulled up beside him at the curb. From the lowered rear window a gloved hand beckons. Einbaum peers around. At the moment he stands alone, so it must be him. "Frau Koenig?" he says, sure that it must be, and he is half into the cab before he knows better. It is a fine scene: Einbaum bodily abducted in the full light of day. This woman in the cab he knows casually from the musical evenings at the Studenten Klub, and from pictures of her in the *Wiener Tagblatt* skiing in the Alps or playing tennis. A peasant, physically, she has wrists and ankles that are thicker and stronger than Einbaum's. Her blue eyes are much too small for her broad, blond face. Not that it mattered; small or not, they had singled out and selected Einbaum. More important to the scene, as time would prove, was the scent, both animal and mineral, into which Einbaum dipped his head. The day was humid. In such weather everything smells. It left the cab with her, however, and Einbaum would come to know it as the *fleur de peur*, the scent of fear that she never lost. Soon enough, alas, everything else would be taken from the Countess Horvath-Szapati but this odor—and Mendelssohn Einbaum. Neither was ever lost.

Was it with this incident that everything of interest might be said to have begun? The summer of 1939, the city of Vienna was like a shabby, unaired museum full of aging attendants and apprehensive tourists, where young men and women of Einbaum's age lived with dreams already buried. Vienna was not music to Einbaum, nor the sight of the bedding of lovers at the casement windows, nor *Kaffee mit Schlag*, nor a dying way of life, nor any of the many things he discussed with his friends or read in the *Neue Wiener Zeitung*. In those days he carried a card engraved with the name of Mendels-sohn Einbaum. He used the tip of his cane to flip leaves from the sidewalk and, with the Countess, a Hungarian from Pest, attended the séances of Lady Golding-Brieslau in her apartment on Schottengasse. Einbaum liked the atmosphere of anxiety, dread, and childish awe. At the ringing of bells his heart pounded. The odor of fear was stronger than the incense. Regardless of what happened, Einbaum himself felt cleansed and one of the chosen to have survived it. He felt he understood the appeal of the Mass without the nonsense of the faith. Besides elderly women, he also met people of unusual background or superior attainments.

Countess Horvath-Szapati played remarkable tennis and had a scholarly interest, like her father, in church history. She spoke, in addition to German and Hungarian, excellent English and French. With a deliberation that was characteristic she used Einbaum to practice her French, skillfully fending off his efforts to practice his English. She talked of going to Brazil. Her father, Count Horvath, had mining interests that would profit from her personal supervision. She had the cunning and assurance of a Cossack. Frizzy straw-colored hair topped her large, round skull, seamlessly joined to her shoulders. Indoors she perspired. In the dimmed light of the séance her face gleamed like gold leaf. All the features were too small, more like those of a child than a woman, the small pointed teeth busily nibbling at her wind-chapped lips. Hardly a beauty or a charmer, the Countess Horvath-Szapati had a somewhat puzzling but magnetic attraction. Her eyes sparkled. Something to do with animal vitality. Einbaum was not alone in the thought he had given to how a man might seduce such a woman, if that was the word. Her thighs were enormous. In her frequent rages at tennis blunders she would snap the racquet in her hands like pastry. What did she want with French? She considered it the language of confidences. Einbaum's inside track, insofar as he had one, lay in his superior knowledge of the French subjunctive. The question of what to *do* with money, for instance, or jewels, seemed amusing and plausible when discussed in French. It was possible to be remarkably intimate, and yet impersonal. French novels were specific, if not up-to-date. There were also imaginary problems of travel, decisions about luggage, and questions of climate. Heat she did not like. Her favorite high place in Europe seemed to be in Gavarnie, in the Pyrenees. One could see it on a poster in the lobby of the American Express. She liked high places. She liked the white silence of a world of snow. Einbaum, in contrast, felt himself especially drawn to lower altitudes and more open space. The American Wild West appealed to Einbaum—what he had seen of it in the movies. Man and nature harmoniously blended. The savage beauty and simplicity of the Indian. In the Historical Museum, Einbaum had paused to examine the feathered headgear of the chiefs, and their bows and arrows. Remote as cavemen, yet alive at the time Einbaum's Grandfather Nottebaum came from Prague to Vienna, the Battle of Balaklava the high point of his long life.

Einbaum loved the movies and felt they were related, in a way, to the séance. One sat in the dark and waited for materializations; at the movies they occurred. To Einbaum's taste, these appearances were more gratifying than the ringing of bells, the table knockings, and the voices that the Countess found so impressive. Although a devout Catholic, she liked the reassurance of a more physical survival. The spiritual she took for granted. No doctrine justified a belief in the spirit's return to the flesh, but she felt there might be progress in this area.

The purpose of religion, quite simply, was to dispense with the problem of death. A start had been made, but fulfillment would come when the spirit recovered the flesh it had lost. Einbaum saw it as part of her primitive, Magyar inheritance. It amused him that this indestructible woman seemed so concerned with her life elsewhere. She wore a jeweled cross, a scarab ring, and carried in her purse cabalistic objects to increase her luck and frighten away evil spirits. To what end? Yet Einbaum noted he felt safer in her company.

As the summer waned, Einbaum helped the Countess shop for what she might need in her travels. It was not clear where; that would be the last decision she would make. He rode about with her in taxis, holding her purchases. In the confines of the cab, if not concealed by the smell of her rubbers, or of her wet coat and umbrella, Einbaum was aware, as in a shuttered sickroom, of the odor of the patient, or the illness. This woman who smelled of money, health, and assurance also gave off the sweet-sour scent of fear. An essence—like that in stoppered bottles—puffed out of her clothes when she sagged into a chair. Was it death she feared? Was she ill with more than apprehension? The straw-yellow hair, the ice-blue eyes, the face as broad and flat as a trowel concealed from others, but not from her, the dram of tainted blood that troubled her thoughts. In diplomatic French she admitted to Einbaum that they had more in common than met the eye. In her father's blood Sophia Kienholz, a Jewess, had left the strain that his daughter, among others, thought apparent. Not anything in particular—no, nothing like that. One simply sensed it was there, as one sensed it in Einbaum. The Jewishness. The *je ne sais quoi*, as the French would say. Einbaum was quick to appreciate the confidence, and share their mutual bond and apprehension. So much for the secretly tainted

Count Horvath. But what did this have to do with the openly tainted Einbaum?

They were in the *Kaffeehaus* frequented by musicians, on the Lindengasse. Einbaum had taken his coffee *mit Schlag*, and sat dunking the puff with his spoon. Conspiracies he liked. In French they ran smoother and promised more reward. In public the Countess frequently wore gloves to conceal the rings embedded in her fingers, but the kid leather fit so snugly it bore a clear imprint of the stones. There had been no discussion about how to conceal the jewels she could not take off. Einbaum was inexperienced, but not indifferent to the nuances and complexities of his emotions. He liked the drama. He vaguely sensed that the drama, with the passage of time, would prove to be of more interest than the crisis. With one gloved finger the Countess Horvath-Szapati pressed her lip to where her teeth could nibble a raw spot, her eyes flickering from side to side to show the charge of her thought. Einbaum was thinking somebody should paint her, regretting that he lacked the talent. This cunning blond peasant disguised as a countess had reason for her apprehension. What reason did she have for Einbaum?

In the opinion of the Countess, Mendelssohn Einbaum bore a remarkable resemblance to Count Horvath. The same stocky frame, with no neck to speak of. The deferent, attentive manner of a good headwaiter. Also a good listener, with an almost inaudible voice. The Count was a student of Ottoman history and spent most of his time living privately, among his books, or hunting in the forests of Abony, the family estate neighboring Pest. He saw few people; outside of family friends, even fewer saw him. If Einbaum, for instance, occupied the Count's quarters—with the knowledge of a few close servants—and went through his usual habits, or stayed in his quarters, he (the Count) might not actually be missed for weeks, possibly months. That would prove to be more than enough time for the Countess and her father, traveling different routes to the same destination, to be in Brazil, Guatemala, Gavarnie, in the Pyrenees, or possibly the Canary Islands, before his absence was noted. Einbaum, in the meantime, would have broken no law and his impersonation would have been purely accidental. As a friend of the Countess, he had been a guest on the estate. He could stay on, or he could return to Vienna as soon as he had received word from the Countess. Einbaum, of course, would do this as a favor, but the Countess would see to it that he was rewarded. One of the rings from her fingers would make it worth his trouble, if that was what it would take.

Had Einbaum forgotten that he, too, was a Jew? Perhaps he had never felt it so strongly. Besides, he was no Horvath and had nothing to lose but his life. In August of 1939, in Vienna, it was hard to imagine who would take Einbaum's. There were laws on the statute books. High in the council of the city of Linz was an influential uncle, husband of an Einbaum. Besides, the minor risks involved appealed to him. Not for nothing had Einbaum been a student of the gangster film and the Wild West.

Einbaum himself made the boat reservations for their trip to Budapest, on the seventh of September. That was the season for river outings, and they were certain to be seen by innumerable people. For this excursion Einbaum bought himself a trenchcoat, of the sort popular with Germans, and a cane often seen at the races, with the handles forming a saddle the observer could sit on. That was not all. The metal shaft contained a glass tube for several ounces of brandy or *kirschwasser*. When it was not in use, he wore it in the crook of his arm.

Thus matters stood on the first day of September, the day Hitler invaded Poland. Just one day later, with a servant named Rudi, who carried several pairs of skis along with other luggage, the Countess and Einbaum took a train for a ski resort in the Italian Alps. They left the train at Graz, however, and went by car to a village on the Hungarian border. Count Horvath, perhaps without luggage, would arrive on the bus that left Pest that morning. He would take Einbaum's seat on the train; Einbaum would return to Pest and they would make new plans. The bus from Pest appeared on schedule, before midnight, but Count Horvath was not on it. A briefcase with his initials, containing a bottle of *akvavit*, two Swiss chocolate bars, and a phial of sleeping powders, was found on one of the seats. Without a word Sophia Szapati took one of her ski poles and beat the driver of the bus as she would a horse. When Einbaum tried to restrain her, she beat him. All of this was observed by the servant Rudi, from his seat on the pile of luggage. He waited both for help and for the seizure to pass. This side of her temperament was new to Einbaum, and so was her grief. Was it her affection for the Count, or merely the interruption of her plans? Nothing would console her. She bolted the door to her room in the inn, but her shoes were there in the morning for Rudi to polish. First things first. Later that day, inanely gay, as if drugged, her mouth frozen in the smile of an animal trainer, she appeared at Einbaum's door to tell him that marriage would simplify their travel problems. Had she lost her mind? The point seemed academic. She still had more mind to lose than Einbaum. Nothing at Einbaum's disposal had the power to deflect her will. There would be delays, thanks to complications, and Einbaum thought he read the script as a staged performance, an act of hysteria that met her needs but for which she might not be responsible later. Shock, they called it. Einbaum would come to know much about shock.

In practical terms, the novels of intrigue supplied them both with a pattern of action. Little seemed new. All of this had been done so often before. Stranger couples than Einbaum and the Countess were seen on trains out of Vienna, and their story would not surprise the porter she had generously tipped. The servant Rudi had been blessed, put on the bus, and sent back to Pest. Strange that Einbaum, rocking in a berth euphoric with *akvavit* and the rising elevation, should remark that he had seldom felt so good about the future at the moment the lights were going out over Europe. How explain it? He was by nature a gentle, even apprehensive, man.

Money got them to Spain. The plane itself, a kite with open cockpits, recruited in Gorizia, was worth less than the money they paid for the passage, but she enjoyed the flight. At a moment her fear, accumulating for hours, would release itself in exhilaration—the thrill of a child rocking the seat of a Ferris wheel. Einbaum was terrified. He sat so long with stiff, clasped hands he had no feeling in his fingers. Wind filled his ears at night. They might have flown on to Lisbon, and from there to New York, but the travel agent could find few listings and accommodations under "Skiing." Before they flew on to Brazil, where little snow fell, the Countess wanted a last winter of skiing, and a chance to reconsider her plans for the future. The war might soon be over. Privately, she feared the godless Russians more than the Germans.

With her two sets of skis and shoe skates for Einbaum —along with wool mittens and matching fur earmuffs— they went north to a village in the Spanish Pyrenees that proved to be jammed with refugee traffic. There was little skiing. There was also a shortage of rooms and beds. The rumor was that ports of exit, in either direction, were in the hands of spies or Nazi sympathizers, and all foreigners, particularly Jews, were subject to investigation, their possessions confiscated. Was it possible? Einbaum thought it possible.

Countess Horvath-Szapati, traveling alone, with the added inducement of a little jewelry, might fly off to do her skiing elsewhere. Then again she might not. Although she was fond, as she said, of Einbaum, and talked to him as she would to a priest, her feelings, as well as her affections, followed the custom of a master and a servant. Frankly, Einbaum rather liked it. It testified to her breeding, as her appearance did not. On the vantage side, for Einbaum, this proved to mean that she needed him more than he needed her. She was accustomed to a Rudi, or a Helga, or a pet—she was subject to weeping for a hound, Süsschen, that slept on her bed and licked her awake—to be there at her side, at her service, or within range of her voice. The division of the men and women made necessary by the crowding—into separate groups, occupying separate dormitories—was a greater hardship on the Countess than the incident at the border. She could not stand the lack of privacy; she could not stand absolute privacy. Without Einbaum she lost her wits. She made a fool of herself among the women, pointing out that she, Sophia Szapati, was a countess, and offering to make it worth the while of those with the taste to recognize it. Women with that sort of taste were not lacking. The Countess's ingroup, a half-dozen or more females he was never given the opportunity to study, occupied a corner of the dormitory screened off from the room with several bedsheets. Among them was a Spanish Jewess, a lean, bitter woman Einbaum thought he might have seen later in the movie *La Strada*—one of the faces uplifted to the performer on the high wire. A cardinal principle of the Countess was that Jews could be bought. She let it be known that she would buy her way out, preferably through France, when the winter was over. She liked the language. She would take up residence in Paris. This should have upset Einbaum or made him apprehensive, but his temperament displayed a chronic weakness: people amazed him. What would they think of next? His anger at human folly was not equal to the pleasure observing it gave him. This remarkable woman, known to him as a countess, could change her spots when the *script* called for it. The word "script" was Einbaum's. It seemed appropriate to the cast and the circumstances. Here in the Pyrenees, as in an ambitious movie, several thousand strangers were locked in a drama of waiting. Einbaum did not merely endure it. No, as the tension mounted, he speculated on its resolution. Along with hunches and calculated guesses, there was increasingly the question of people. Like francs, pesetas, and dollars, they were negotiable. Some would prove to cash in, others to check out. As an example, the Countess, for all her discomfort, was at her best when she *hated* something. That she had in abundance. It brought out in her a vitality, a passion, that Einbaum associated with more intimate matters. This cow of a woman aroused desire. Einbaum marked it in himself. She slept in the clothes she feared she might lose, with her valuables worn on a chain at her armpit. Einbaum had seen them, green as American money, when she raised her arms to put up her hair. Someone had told her this patina would increase their value, testifying to their age. Cash money she kept in a fold of flesh at her waist.

One morning at sunrise, the village still in the shadow of the snowcapped peaks to the east, Einbaum was awakened by a boy, Alexis, and hurriedly taken to the women's quarters. Most of them slept. There had been no disturbance to wake them up. The stale air had the sickening sweetness Einbaum associated with the female period. In the favored location, for which she had paid, set off from the cots of her ingroup, Sophia Szapati sprawled on her back as if stoned. A wet towel had been placed on her forehead and eyes, but her mouth stood open. In such a bulk, how small it looked. A quilt pressed between her flanks, where someone had kneeled. Among other things too numerous to mention, the Countess Szapati had lost the gold crowns to her teeth. Someone had propped open the jaws, fished them out. Einbaum had the impression of a crudely looted piece of antique statuary, known to have had rare gems for eyes and solid gold teeth. Nevertheless, the overall impression was comical. A beached and looted hulk, or ship's prow, waiting for the tide to sweep it out to sea. The ring promised to Einbaum had been cunningly cut from her finger. On her spacious behind—she had been rolled on her face by an official who knew what to look for, and where—a spot no larger than a pinprick indicated the point where the needle had entered. Perhaps it had never left. (Einbaum had heard the stories of how they circulated like fish in the bloodstream.) This grotesque incident would not have occurred in the orderly rigor of a well-run police state, and owed its success to the relaxed confusion of the time and place. Friends and enemies were not clearly defined—a situation she instinctively feared. The consensus was that she had been the victim of the impression she left on others. Nothing would kill her. So she had had the benefit of too great a dose. The frail and cunning were better qualified to survive.

Einbaum's health actually improved on the camp rations and absence of tobacco. The letters Einbaum might have written for himself he wrote for others in French, German, and English. Few were answered. Einbaum was not tempted to try his luck. The past so desperately cherished by others held little attraction for him. Nor did the flight to Brazil, Canada, or the United States. Confinement gratified something in his temperament. An elderly Jew, Klugmann, who asked Einbaum's help with his Double-Crostics, diagnosed Einbaum's contentment as a return to the womb of the ghetto. Here in the camp he was at home. In a condition of freedom was he ill at ease? Klugmann had practiced psychoanalysis in Prague, where the anxiety of the Jews, if they had not been dispersed by war and incineration, would have tested Klugmann's theory that fear was more productive of spiritual renewal than hope. Now it hung in the air. Klugmann talked in this way while Einbaum dozed over the gaps in Klugmann's Double-Crostics—an American entertainment supplied to him by the secretary of the American Friends Service Committee, a society of Quakers. The Crostics came to her from a friend in New York by the name of Bettina Gernsprecher. It was Einbaum who took the trouble to write and thank her for them both.

Here is Einbaum in New York. A greeting-card salesman, he has the use of one of the company's imported Volvos. The president is a Swede, a strong believer in foreign trade. Einbaum's area is in Bucks County, where his knowledge of German is considered an advantage. His manner is friendly, but his speech is sort of muttering, and the talk slacks off. There is something annoying about Einbaum, but it goes unmentioned, being hard to define. What is appealing is obvious. Einbaum is human. He has lived, like you, an already long and pointless life. He is on the road four or five days a week, and looks forward to sleeping late on Sundays. While in the city Einbaum stays with Bettina Gernsprecher, who colors the greeting cards by hand. The outline is there, and

Bettina is free to vary the colors of the lips, the hair, and the eyes. This costs the buyer extra, but it gives Bettina a steady job. It takes eight months of the year to prepare for the seasonal rushes. Bettina sits on a stool, her back arched over so the bones protrude like knuckles, her knees drawn up to support the clipboard and the card. She puts a point to the brush by twisting it on her lips. Einbaum has warned her. He has told her the story of the women who died from painting numerals on watch faces —those that glow in the dark. Bettina's cards do not glow as yet, but one day they might. On his trips to the city Einbaum brings her his laundry, and while they listen to music she darns his socks. She likes to darn. She cannot sit for long without using her hands.

Early pictures of Bettina are lacking, since they were destroyed with the ghetto in Cracow. Because she was tall for her age, a place was made for her in a brothel limited to Jewish females. This information she shared with Einbaum the Sunday they went to the Met together. Humiliation, remorse, even self-disgust are sentiments that she has dispensed with. There is skill in her hands. She received her training in a concentration camp. She paid her own way when Einbaum took her to lunch, and shared with him the lower half of her daybed. Stretched at his side, or beneath him, she was taller, but her chronic stoop brought her eye to eye with him in elevators. Einbaum saw very little of her when they walked in the street. He found himself, soon enough, either a stride or two behind her or several strides ahead and pausing to wait for her. During her formative years, she had either been led (she found it hard to remember) or pushed from behind.

It is not easily explained that a woman's age and appearance seem irrelevant. Einbaum talked a good deal; could it be said she listened? When Einbaum showered, he would find looped over the curtain rail her brassiere with the padded cups: if a woman really cared *that* much, why didn't she care more? Another time he found a shirt that was not his own in the laundry he brought back from the city. A small neck size, but the arms of an ape. Einbaum returned the shirt without comment, and that was where the matter rested.

Nevertheless, in her company he was subject to puzzling sensations. Years after any woman had been seen with a bob, Bettina found it a sensible hair style. The hair in front she cut herself, and let the barber apply clippers at the back. Einbaum could not make up his mind if he thought her a new and higher form of life or a lower. Her detachment extended beyond the things of this world. It was the contrary—he felt obliged to point out—with Sophia Szapati, the other woman in his life. She had been attached to things until death and thieves took them from her. "Looted" was the word. Einbaum had frequently described the spectacle for Bettina. The puzzling thing was that these two women, for all their differences, had one thing in common. They had chosen Einbaum. It could not be said that he had actually chosen them. Sophia had all but kidnapped him in Vienna, beckoning to him from the back seat of the taxi, and Bettina Gernsprecher, sight unseen, had agreed to support him until he found work, persuading her employer with the ape-long arms to hire Einbaum as a greeting-card salesman.

So here is Einbaum—through, as we say, no fault of his own.

1971

Drrdla

The house needed painting when the Fechners acquired it, and Walter rented the equipment necessary to do it, climbing like a fireman to get at the rafters high in the gables. Inside, both the floors and the woodwork had been covered with many coats of paint. Walter removed it all to bring out the natural beauty of the wood. Light streamed through the high first-floor windows that Walter had cleaned with professional equipment. Whatever Walter undertook to do, he did professionally. In three of the upstairs rooms he installed cypress paneling obtained for a song from a demolition company, at the same time installing insulation materials that kept the summer heat out, the winter heat in. So much for first things first. In the dark months of the winter he taught himself to paint—among other things grinding his own colors—and with his wife Hanna's assistance, he took up the study of the cello. If it was largely a matter of application, Walter knew how to apply himself. He did no more than what he could, provided the day was long enough.

Hanna had "found" him in a jeweler's shop in Kussnacht, directly across the lake from Lucerne. His job had been to polish the silver and keep hundreds of cuckoo clocks cuckooing. They covered one solid wall of the shop into which Hanna had stepped to buy herself a new watchband, the pendulums rocking, the birds cuckooing, in one insane instant happening. The sight had so affected Hanna she had closed her eyes. Walter had spoken to her. Then another year passed before she returned, having made up her mind it was Walter she wanted.

One could hardly believe that to look at Hanna, a scholarly, shy-seeming, very Swiss woman. It had been her decision. Perhaps her being older than Walter persuaded him to let her make it. He was so very much the man Hanna knew that she wanted, it was not necessary for her to be his ideal woman. That proved to be acceptable to Walter because women were not one of his major interests. He liked them, but he didn't need them. What he proved to need, after six years of marriage, was an intelligent, congenial male companion. That was Herman Lewin. He had been recruited with this in mind. Lewin badly needed a place to stay while he completed his medical studies. Walter's knowledge of German was a help to Lewin, and he in turn tutored Walter in the new analytic psychology. If the war came up, as it sometimes did, it was discussed in an open, intelligent manner. Herman Lewin was Jewish. Hanna and Walter

Fechner were German-Swiss. They were all agreed that German culture could not be held responsible for a few madmen, anymore than all Americans could be held responsible for Huey Long.

"I tell you what," Hanna would say, lowering her cup with a clack to her saucer. "You men are all crazy. It's a *man's* crazy world." Hanna simply couldn't help, on occasion, showing her resentment for a man-run world. In Switzerland a woman did not have the right to vote, no matter how smart she was. In America she could teach, but not look forward to the usual promotions. A doddering idiot could head the department of German literature—as he now did—if his sex was male.

Hanna was not the lighthearted, uncomplicated person that Lewin had assumed from their exchange of letters. She had her moods. They made her, surely, more interesting. Like the night-light at the top of the stairs, she was either turned on, or she was turned off. Her work at the college demanded all of her strength, and she turned on for the college as she closed the door of the house behind her, and walked down the steps. In the way she strode off, carrying her stuffed valise, Lewin recognized the European in exile. Her pride and status tipped her slightly backward. The American who walked behind tipped slightly forward, forging ahead. In the late afternoon Hanna's return to the house was signaled by a loud clapping of her hands. A professor might do that to waken sleeping pupils. In this way Hanna summoned Walter and Lewin to tea. She would have changed her dress, and her face would be free of the light touch of makeup she wore to college. The tea hour permitted Hanna to enjoy at home some of the pleasures of supervision that were part of teaching. It was Hanna who spooned the tea from the pewter canister: Hanna who timed the steeping: and Hanna who poured—glancing up to check with Lewin, who sometimes varied, as to the number of lumps of sugar he wanted. Walter was allowed to slice up the *kuchen*. Hanna judged the strength of the tea by its odor, an exercise that left a film of steam on her glasses. Much of this vexed Walter. To avoid the fuss, he might not appear until his tea was poured and cooling. An unsuspected side of Hanna's nature was revealed in the way she attacked her food. As if famished. Utterly absorbed until she was fed. Her way of opening her mouth, wide, then closing it with a birdlike chomp was disturbing. Later, with a finger moistened at her lips, she would peck around the table picking up crumbs, scraps of nuts, cake, and icing. Into her appetite Hanna put a great deal of living. The strong brew of tea gave her pale face a flush and started, as she said, "her motor running." As a rule it would run for about two hours. This animated Hanna was capable of "glee"—something new in Lewin's experience. She would give herself over, quite completely, to the humor of something Lewin had mentioned, not infrequently placing her hand on his arm, or as high as his shoulder, and applying astonishing pressure. The violin, she said, had done much to strengthen her hands.

Whatever Hanna believed to be so funny was invariably lost on Walter. He would sit waiting for her fit of humor to pass. Loose strands of her hair would cling to her lips, and tears of glee give a shine to her eyes. "If it's so amusing," Walter would say, "I fail to understand why you can't explain it." That she couldn't, of course, was what she found so amusing, and made matters worse. Minutes after such a scene at the table she might be heard giggling at the sink in the kitchen, or almost choking with laughter in her study. Walter put it down as a characteristic female symptom. Women were strange creatures, in Walter's opinion, still at the whimsical mercy of the moon's orbit. He detected, and complained of, the odor in the house during Hanna's "lunar period," during which time he took his shower in a stall he had erected in the basement. The basement smelled of nothing worse than fertilizer and hibernating plants.

Walter had a peasant's blunt directness of manner, but Lewin considered him rustically handsome. A woman might like him, although most objects were prone to bend or break in his hands. The handles snapped off cups, or broke off utensils, if Walter was asked to wash or dry them. His large-knuckled hands were those of a man half again his size. He broke off wine corks, snapped off pipestems, bent the prongs of forks as he mashed potatoes, and invariably cut so deep into the cheese board Lewin was warned to beware of splinters. In the basement, in fact, broken into fragments, were many mail-order objects he had tried to assemble. The iron legs of a new-type collapsible bed were twisted as if some monster had seized them. He snapped buttons off the collars of his shirts and the flies of his pants. It was of course impossible for him to shave without cutting himself. From the back and side his large knobby head resembled the Swiss carvings used for bottle stoppers, but his eyes were intelligent, and his voice, as a rule, pleasant. His gestures, however, in a heated discussion, were more like those of a karate expert, the flat of his hand slicing right or left, or brought down like a cleaver into his palm. It had not been easy for such a man to turn to painting, the cello, and the touch system of typing. The typing went the slowest, since the machine was usually in need of repair.

Walter's paintings were largely an excuse for making handsome frames. He drilled the wormholes by hand, and applied his own antique finish. These canvases were painted at the second-floor windows and demonstrated his mastery of perspective. No painting had been done out of the house. Walter did not like the curious gazing at him, or confusing him with some bohemian-type artist. All he was doing was showing what a man could do if he applied himself. He gave the pictures numbers, and signed himself Fechner where the signature was not obtrusive. He meant to say no more than that he was responsible for what he had made.

Lewin was still in bed, on a Sunday morning, when Walter rapped on his door. He came in with flecks of sawdust in his hair and a thick powder of the dust on his hands. It was common to see Walter Fechner heated— by work he did with his hands, or the warmth of his emotions—but Lewin had never before seen him excited. It changed the pitch of his voice. He looked both foolish and appealing. "It's there!" he said.

Lewin said, "What?"

Walter shrugged in the European manner, spreading his hands.

"What is where?" Lewin repeated.

Walter replied, "The basement!" He spoke in a hushed, gruff whisper, as if someone were listening. Music thundered to a climax in Hanna's room. "It's there!" he said again, and Lewin was pleased to see, for himself, what Hanna had once seen in Walter. A boy's wide-eyed startled pleasure in a man's face. So what had happened? Walter had been at work at his bench, cutting a piece of glass. He had reached that stage where the glass had to be tapped with the tool to break it: a tingling sound is given off as it splinters. In the silence that followed this high-pitched vibration he heard a sound in the timbers behind him. That part of the basement was little more than an air space between the floor of the kitchen and the foundation. Old boards were piled there. Also a few traps in case of rats. There was no access to the basement from the yard, but Walter had found rat turds on his workbench. They were uncanny, those fellows. Walter had for them the highest respect.

His first thought was that he had caught a rat, and the creature, in pain, had made this sound. So he used a flashlight to check the traps back in the darkness. Both had been sprung, and the bait was gone. Otherwise nothing. He had stood there for some time, lost in thought. When he returned to work he picked up the glass and finished off what he had started. Once more, as the glass splintered, he had heard the sound. How describe it? Something between a peep and a squeak. So he took the trouble to clear away the boards and aim the beam of the flashlight into the corners. At the farthest point, the way a distant road sign picks up the glint of the headlights, he saw—for a moment he saw—two eyes: glasslike splinters of chill went up and down his spine. The palm of the hand that gripped the light had filmed with sweat. The primeval, ur-fears of man needed only this spinal tingle to revive them. Eyes gleaming in a cavelike darkness. Sounds that were felt as much as they were heard.

What had Walter done? At the moment nothing. He had been paralyzed. Sometime later he had aimed the beam of spotlight into the darkest corner. Walter and this creature had just stared at each other. A bat, possibly? No, the head was too large. In Walter's experience it resembled the slender loris, a bizarre creature he had seen only in books. A head that appeared all eyes. Fearing to damage eyes so long accustomed to darkness Walter had switched off the light and come straight to Lewin. What did he want? What he wanted from Lewin was advice.

That he thought he would get it from Lewin was a measure of his confusion. Lewin's feeling about anything found in basements was not one of excitement.

Why else had he picked an apartment in the attic if not to get as far as possible from basements? Anything that slithered, squirmed, or dragged a tail was not, for Lewin, an object of study. But that was not yet known. Whatever it was, it had not yet moved. Lewin's advice—since Walter stood there, waiting—was to lure the creature into the open. Put down food and water. Put down anything the poor devil might eat. In a picture magazine Lewin had once seen a beast all eyes and ears, like a giant Mickey Mouse.

"That's a loris," said Walter, and in that simple manner he recovered his sense of proportion. It was not really advice he wanted or needed from Lewin—just his reassurance.

He did take Lewin's tip about the food, and put down samples of cheese, meat and nuts, and canned fish. Also cereals, dry and cooked. What happened? Nothing. Nor did it respond to the bait of warm milk. That would have settled the matter for Lewin, but it merely increased the challenge for Walter. He prepared more fish, both fresh and canned mackerel, and pushed the tin plate of food back into the darkness. The next morning he could see that the mackerel had been licked clean of the sauce. More sauce was added, and this too licked off. Was it only the sauce that it liked, or did it lack the strength, or the teeth, to chew with? Walter asked Lewin, whose teeth were not so good. So that the creature could gum the fish, if necessary, a pulpy soup was made of the mackerel. That helped. The loris proved to have a weakness for canned fish soup.

From the basement stairs, where Walter kept his vigil, he used mirrors to keep his eyes on the food plate. A dim, indirect light, from a shaded bulb, transformed the scene into a parched, barren landscape. In this tableau a rat would loom as large as a dinosaur. At its farthest rim, all ears and popped eyes, a creature gazed toward Walter with a fish-smeared snout, then turned, like a reptile, and squirmed off. The tail it dragged was thin and long as a rat's, but covered with fur. If Walter could believe his eyes he had seen a starved cat. Fortunately, for Lewin, he would have to wait until the creature had gained both courage and substance. This would take time. Lewin had to gain a little courage himself.

Walter began with liquid vitamins smeared on the fish or dropped into the saucer of canned milk. Quite simply, the creature had to learn to both chew food and digest it. Like a healthy cat choking on a fur ball, it had to swallow, and gag, then swallow again. Walter was patient. He spoke words of comfort and encouragement. In return it might make the sound suggested by the word drrrdla, with a rolling of the r's. Not a mew, or a meow, but a sound that looked forward—as Walter put it—to being a real mew someday. Drrdla. For the moment it served as a name. If Walter made a move in its direction it would squirm like a reptile into the darkness, but if he made only coaxing, catlike noises it was not disturbed. When Lewin came down for breakfast he would find Walter on the basement stairs, off the landing, a flashlight in his lap and a pair of bird glasses on a strap about his neck.

"How's your friend?" Lewin would ask.

"She's coming," Walter would reply, although the matter of sex was still undetermined. Her color, from what he could tell, had once been gray and white.

What it all came down to, in Walter's opinion, was the emergence of life from darkness. God knows where the creature had come from, or what had been the cause of its terror, but it now slowly squirmed its way from the primeval past into the present. It had managed to live, like a hibernating plant, on snatches of light. The very

73

idea of a friendly gesture, or an upward look, had not emerged into its consciousness. What Walter found on his hands was a creature, like man, that had fallen from grace. Some blind or deliberate moment of terror had erased its mind of all experience. A *tabula rasa*. It had to begin, once more, from scratch. Would it be possible to restore such a fallen creature to normal life? If possible, Walter would do it. In that simple animal, as in man, there was a hunger for human affection: in its tiny, wounded soul it was drawn toward the light it feared. Like some people, it had lived in darkness so long it found the presence of light painful. The parallels were endless. The challenge inexhaustible. No project Walter had previously undertaken tested, at once, so many of his talents. Commitment and patience. Walter would prove to have what the challenge required. Every day he modified, in some way, the approach he used to win her over. It was the talk she liked: a very womanly aspect of her temperament. To enlarge his range Walter used a birdcall that employed a piece of metal in a wooden disc. What sounds he made! How her eyes would widen, her large, batlike ears would twitch. This could be observed from the landing of the stairs without intruding on her privacy. Lewin observed it. A head (he did not say so) like those withered specimens on women's fur pieces, with gems for eyes. Hanna preferred to wait, as she said, until it looked more like a cat than a rodent. That would take time. Out of long habit the creature crawled rather than walked.

Just living in the dark had developed, in Drrdla, faculties that most cats had learned to do without. Her eyes, for example, were not to be trusted. She relied on other, subtler, signals. It was not out of the question that a room full of light would blind her as badly as total darkness. Take such a simple thing as perspective. How it was that objects, in *her* space, related to her. What was near and far, up and down. How high she could leap. How far she could fall. The blind woman, Helen Keller, had learned to live in a world that had no dimensions whatsoever. Drrdla was not so handicapped, but neither was she so smart. To make her way back to normal life she had to recover much of what she had lost, as well as discover faculties that were new to cats. If she made it, she would be a sort of cat-genius, starting from scratch. If one was fond of cats it could be depressing how dumb they were in simple situations, but it was inspiring what they could do when the going was tough. Few had ever had tougher going than Drrdla, if she proved to be tough enough.

The lyrical side of Walter's nature, not previously displayed, revealed a faculty that he had allowed to languish. Circumstance now required that he exercise it to an unusual degree, at breakfast. In these discussions Lewin had a glimpse of the rough diamond Hanna had plucked from the bed of cuckoo clocks. In these moments the knob-headed, iron-handed peasant underwent a transformation. Why not? Wasn't that just what he was pointing out? Evolution itself, he told Lewin, had surely come about in just this manner. This kind of thinking, of course, went around and around, and that was how Walter went. Around and around. Lewin watched and listened, sometimes risking what he felt to be a pertinent observation. What if this creature finally made it? Became a plain, normal cat. Both Hanna and Walter had once and for all decided not to be the victims of pets: it was pets that had people. It was pets that determined their lives. Wouldn't this cat, when it *lived* in the house, be some sort of pet? Walter said that such a prospect was so far away he hadn't given it serious consideration. One thing at a time. The thing at the moment was the basement wall.

This low cement wall, about waist-high, divided Drrdla's territory from the rest of the basement. She would come to the edge of it, no further, to nibble her fish. If Walter moved the plate to his workbench, or the floor, there it would sit through the night untouched. This wall, in short, provided her with the line that simplified decisions. From its edge she would crouch and exchange glances with Walter. What did he want? What did he now expect of *her?* This confronted Walter with a dilemma he was not in a position to answer. What *did* he want—besides just wanting her to come out? Suppose she really felt more at her ease with the life she had? Food enough, now, on the one hand: and all that privacy on the other. What—her glance seemed to ask—did he have in mind?

In Walter's opinion the problem was aggravated by the apparent increase of noise. Doors slammed. Was this something new, or had he merely not noticed it so much in the past? At his vigil in the basement these jarring blasts rattled the house like an earth tremor. Was it necessary? Hanna couldn't seem to gather what the trouble was. Had it reached the point, she asked, where entering and leaving her very own house created a disturbance? Would he like her to pad around the house barefoot, leaving her shoes at the door like a Japanese? Was it all right if she listened to music in the evening, and was awakened in the morning by her alarm? If just her living in the house disturbed his *little rodent*, perhaps she should think of taking a room elsewhere. Plainly, Walter and the cat couldn't, living, as they did, in such perfect harmony in the basement. Walter hardly knew which disturbed him more, the unpredictable and shattering slam of a door, or the tireless and deliberate way she referred to the creature as his "little rodent."

"How is Walter's little rodent?" she would ask Lewin, first making certain that Walter was within hearing. As aggravating, and even more of a nuisance, was the clattering ring of the phone. An especially loud ring had been installed so that it might be heard both upstairs and in the basement. The cat was naturally startled by the ring, and the way Walter turned and ran up the stairs. What were these calls? He was often just a moment too late to hear. Other times Hanna would like to know if there was something *they* would like at the market, fish or liver, perhaps? What could Walter do? If he allowed his irritation to show, the phone would ring ten minutes later. Both Walter and Hanna had been insistent on having an unlisted number, but now he received calls from solicitors and pollsters. The telephone company could not help him. Hanna would not torment herself trying to learn a new number, after so many years of mastering the old one. To tell him *that*, she phoned.

There were other things: doors were left ajar so a draft would bang them; the thermostat was jiggled on the hot-water heater, resulting in explosive bangs in the heating system. Lewin tried to point out that Walter's suspicions, seen objectively, were without foundation. Doors often slammed; anyone with a phone was sometimes driven almost crazy by it. Circumstance—not Hanna—had made him just a wee bit paranoid. Living in the basement, all ears, like the cat, had given him the feeling that the house was against him. That was almost as silly as Hanna behaving in a jealous manner. Was she crazy?—Walter wanted to know. Jealous of a cat? Lewin suggested that both cats and women had this lunatic side to their natures. They were possessed, so to speak. They would eat or not eat, hide in the darkness or spend the night wailing. They were at once affectionate, trusting, and suspicious of every movement. Idio-cy ruled the world of men—the personal, the separate, the distinct, et cetera—while luna-cy permeated the world of women, their nature subject to forces, and impulses, not easily controlled.

A student of Hanna's, Emil Lubke, who majored in German literature and the piano, was given the key to the house so that he could practice on the idle Fechner piano. Did Walter mind? No, he was free to go for long walks. It took hours of patient, loving coaxing, however, to lure the poor cat, Drrdla, back to the light after two solid hours of Rachmaninoff and Liszt. She now accepted—possibly she even needed—the merest touch of his outstretched hand. Her posture was wary. The tremor in her legs was like that of a kitten with the rickets. All along her bony spine the hairs lifted, and her ears might flatten at the slightest disturbance. It was not unusual for her to cuff him, or with her fangs showing make the hiss of a dragon. This involuntary behavior embarrassed them both, but encouraged a fresh beginning. Palpable to his touch was the muted tremor of her purr. Another thing she couldn't help. The poor creature was torn, in Walter's opinion, between the two great forces that move the world—including the moon. The desire to open out, to confront what is new, and the fear that dictated withdrawal. Vulnerable. The deep fear of being vulnerable. Irresistibly she stretched toward Walter's hand, the mysterious gratification of his touch, and yet an equally compulsive force lured her back into the comforts of darkness. Walter dare not advance, nor make other moves associated with the food plate, but it was clear she *preferred*, after eating, completing her toilet while seated near him. If he remained, she would crouch and take her nap. A puzzling detail was that she always did this with her back to him, her head toward the darkness. Her ears carefully screened his movements, but it did seem a symbolic gesture. It was now Walter *and* Drrdla, against the unknown. Walter could therefore be excused the glance of witless delight he gave Lewin when she allowed him, in Lewin's presence, to scratch her ears. This silent colloquy brought to mind lovers otherwise speechless with emotion. Little wonder that Hanna never seemed to find the time to see how the pair of them were doing. Did she know? As well as she seemed to know the exact moment to startle them both out of their wits. At the electric moment that Walter's finger left the tingling chill of her nose—the phone would ring, a door would slam, or the pipes that ran along the basement ceiling would be convulsed with a pulsing throb, caused by the clever manipulation of the hot-water taps in the bathroom. If both were turned on suddenly, and full, the plumbing pounded like a sick monster. The cat, Drrdla, would disappear. Walter would sit there in the dark, his head in his hands.

If he continued to sit there long enough, however, he would hear, in the shelter of the steps, the drag of her tongue on a patch of her pelt, a sign that she had recovered and in no way held him responsible. He supplemented her diet with wheat-germ oil cunningly smeared on fresh chicken livers. She preferred canned milk to fresh cream, and liked nothing better than to gnaw on colossal-size non-pitted olives. She growled like a tiger when her teeth struck the stone. An olive rolled across the floor and caught her, so to speak, with her guard down. She leaped and pounced. Very peculiar behavior for a sick cat. Equally intimate and peculiar was her lust for the rind of a melon. Walter had left his breakfast slice on the step to gallop up the stairs and answer the phone: when he returned the rind had been chewed away at both ends. Other specialties included peanut butter, cream cheese on a bagel, and cold matzo ball soup. Anything but mice, was Hanna's comment. There *were* a few mice—they rustled wastebasket paper and ate the nuts out of the candy on Hanna's desk—but Walter pointed out this would be taken care of when Drrdla had the run of the house. The remark slipped out. He hadn't meant to go so far, so fast. Hanna made no comment, but a day later he found the basement door propped open. She picked the following weekend to repot most of her plants. This took all of Saturday, and with the racket and confusion Walter saw nothing at all of Drrdla. Hanna also filled the house with fall leaves and dried arrangements, the doors slamming as she went in and out, not to mention the search for bowls and containers in all corners of the basement. Walter himself took one of his long, joyless walks, a McIntosh apple swelling his pocket. Now and then he could hear, wind-borne, the roar of the crowd at the Army–Navy game. The lights were on in the house when he returned, and the door of the kitchen was still propped open. To air out the smell of fertilizer two kitchen windows were propped up from the bottom. Hanna lay soaking in the tub. Walter put out a fresh plate of food for the cat while he scrambled some eggs for himself. Eggs too she liked. But that night she touched nothing on her plate. Walter coaxed her for an hour, then he took the flashlight and probed the corners she usually retired to. Nothing doing. He went from room to room and from the top of the house to the bottom. He discussed the disappearance for some time with Lewin. However improbably, it was possible that she had come up the stairs to the kitchen and gone through the door or one of the windows. What else?

Walter spent the evening circling the block. It was not one of those streets with alleys, so all he could do was stop and peer up the driveways, making those sounds that caused other cats to howl and strange dogs to bark.

The following day Walter moved a cot from the basement to the kitchen. If he heard a cat mewing at the door he would be there, handy, to let the creature in. Part of each night Walter might make a tour of the house. Lying there on the cot he would think of a closet, or some nook or cranny a cat might crawl into, and having thought of it he would have to get up and look. He came up with the bizarre idea that she might have gone up the fireplace. He felt it explained the sprinkle of soot he often heard at night. Naturally, it meant no more fires were started, and at night a dish of food was left on the hearth, just in case. How was one to know just where she might be, until she reappeared? The smell of fish permeated the house. Walter felt obliged to change it daily, making sure it was fresh.

Hanna complained to Lewin that Walter's prowling deprived her of sleep. Her own door she kept locked, with a rug at the bottom, unless she heard Lewin passing. On an equal-time basis, Lewin felt obliged to listen to her side of the story. That too was a long one. Hanna had grown thinner, or rather leaner, but it seemed more appropriate to her role. Her fingers were always nervously laced together, or gripping the arm or the back of a chair. When she spoke to Walter she would always get to her feet. With a chair between them—her hands gripping its back—she would read him one of her "lectures." She was relieved, she told him, that the poor little rodent had managed to escape. It was not being saved for itself at all, but was being held a captive creature by Walter. What the poor cat hungered for was not food, but the company of its own kind. If that was not true it would

81

still be in the basement fattening on chicken liver and Walter's attention. What it wanted, and finally got, was a chance to escape.

Lewin very much admired the way Walter would sit and listen to Hanna as if he felt he had it coming. Walter said it did her good to "blow her top." He put in his time fencing off those areas in the basement where a cat might hide. The night the cat came home Hanna was in bed with a slight flu. Lewin went down alone to the door of the kitchen where he watched, unobserved, the shabby gray-and-white cat gulping up canned mackerel. Was it Drrdla? Spotted gray-and-white cats look pretty much alike. Her splotched white patches were uniformly soiled. Lewin seemed to recall the ears as larger, the tail longer and thinner, but in point of fact he had seldom seen her. His picture of the cat had been formed by Walter's numberless descriptions.

"It's her," Walter said, putting his finger to her head. "I can feel her mew." It was a fact that the cat proved to be curious about the basement, and seemed responsive to the name Drrdla. A final proof would have been a strip of melon rind, but melons were not in season. Walter had also stopped buying the large unpitted olives and had only the green ones, stuffed with pimentos, one of the few things she had tried to bury after sniffing it.

A place was prepared for the cat in the kitchen—a box for sleeping, and a litter box for business—but when Walter came down in the morning she was gone. He searched the house. The cat was finally found asleep at the foot of Hanna's unmade bed. After eating, it was back at her door, where it howled until it gained entrance. There it was when Hanna returned from school, and she thought nothing of it. "Hello, cat," she said. She was not surprised that so smart a cat would rather sleep with her than alone in the kitchen. Why not? It merely showed how sensible she was. The litter box was then moved to Hanna's room since the cat also preferred to spend the day there. The windows were warm and sunny. The place she loved to sleep was on old theme papers in Hanna's wastebasket. Nor did it come as a surprise to Hanna that the cat put on weight in an alarming manner, or chose the top drawer of her bureau—the one with old stockings—to bear and nurse a litter of four kittens, two of them black. During the long day Hanna was not in the room they could be heard doing what four kittens like to do. Walter was kept busy emptying the litter box, and trying to spade up frozen earth in the snow-covered garden. The names of the kittens were Eenie, Meenie, Miney and Moe. Miney and Moe were black. Hanna sometimes carried Moe to the college, in her muff, where he slept in her desk drawer, or played with an eraser. The mother cat, once her work was done, proved to be loose and immoral in her ways. She would howl from room to room, and from floor to floor, until Walter got up and let her out. A night or two later she would howl from door to door until he let her in. Why didn't Hanna complain? She seemed to think it perfectly normal behavior. Once a cat had learned what real life was like, what did Walter expect? Hadn't it been Walter's idea in the first place to help her to develop her faculties? To restore her to grace? Like some people, she had lived in the darkness so long the light of day almost made her giddy. Hanna knew how she felt.

Hanna was scandalized when Walter brought up the idea of having the mother cat fixed. What would he think of next?—she wanted to know. He helped her weigh the cat on the bathroom scale for the first alarming signs of increase. At that point she will need more riboflavin, as it says in the book. Walter was sometimes up four or five times a night letting her in, and then letting her out. It is perfectly plain she now abuses his concern: what can he do? The sound of his padding up and down the stairs keeps Lewin awake. For some time Lewin has been sleeping in a larger bed, and it is Hanna who lies there beside him. Sometimes she giggles. Other times she laughs hysterically. It was this sound that led Lewin to think she was sobbing, and why he opened the door to her room. She beckoned to him. Catlike, he proved open to suggestion. If a laughing fit comes on her late at night she controls it by pressing her face to her pillow. The howling of the toms will bring a flood of laugh tears to her eyes. It is Hanna's back that Lewin feels he knows the best. After her pleasure, like a cat, she shows him her back. Lewin lets his fingers glide along her spine, which seems to him as bony as that of Drrdla, the fuzz of hair along it rising, the back arching, as when Walter first extended his hand toward the dark. If he had then withdrawn it, an unawakened, famished cat still would be captive in the basement, and neither Walter nor Lewin would have on their hands a female creature awakened to life.

1969

A Fight Between a White Boy and a Black Boy in the Dusk of a Fall Afternoon in Omaha, Nebraska

How did it start? If there is room for speculation, it lies in how to end it. Neither the white boy nor the black boy gives it further thought. They stand, braced off, in the cinder-covered schoolyard, in the shadow of the darkened, red-brick building. Eight or ten smaller boys circle the fighters, forming sides. A white boy observes the fight upside down as he hangs by his knees from the iron rail of the fence. A black girl pasting cutouts of pumpkins in the windows of the annex seems unconcerned. Fights are not so unusual. Halloween and pumpkins come but once a year.

At the start of the fight there was considerable jeering and exchange of formidable curses. The black boy was much better at this part of the quarrel and jeered the feebleness of his opponent's remarks. The white boy lacked even the words. His experience with taunts and scalding invective proved to be remarkably shallow. Twice the black boy dropped his arms as if they were useless against such a potato-mouthed, stupid adversary. Once he laughed, showing the coral roof of his mouth. In the shadow of the school little else stood out clearly for the white boy to strike at. The black boy did not have large whites to his eyes, or pearly white teeth. In the late afternoon light he made a poor target except for the shirt that stood out against the fence that closed in the school. He had rolled up the sleeves and opened the collar so that he could breathe easier and fight better. His black bare feet are the exact color of the cinder yard.

The white boy is a big, hulking fellow, large for his age. It is not clear what it might be, since he has been in the same grade for three years. The bottom board has been taken from the drawer of his desk to allow for his knees. Something said about that may have started the quarrel, or the way he likes to suck on toy train wheels. (He blows softly and wetly through the hole, the wheel at the front of his mouth.) But none of that is clear; all that is known is that he stands like a boxer, his head ducked low, his huge fists doubled before his face. He stands more frontally than sidewise, as if uncertain which fist to lead with. As a rule he wrestles. He would much rather wrestle than fight with his fists. Perhaps he refused to wrestle with a black boy, and *that* could be the problem. One never knows. Who ever knows for sure what starts a fight?

The black boy's age hardly matters and it doesn't show. All that shows clearly is his shirt and the way he stands. His head looks small because his shoulders are so wide. He has seen pictures of famous boxers and stands with his left arm stretched out before him as if approaching something in the darkness. His right arm, cocked, he holds as if his chest pained him. Both boys are hungry, scared, and waiting for the other one to give up.

The white boy is afraid of the other one's blackness, and the black boy hates and fears whiteness. Something of their mutual fear is now shared by those who are watching. One of the small black boys hoots like an Indian and takes off. One of the white boys has a pocketful of marbles he dips his hand into and rattles. This was distracting when the fight first started, and he was asked to take his hands out of his pockets. Now it eases the strain of the silence.

The need to take sides has also dwindled, and the watchers have gathered with the light behind them, out of their eyes. They say "Come on!" the way you say "sic 'em," not caring which dog. A pattern has emerged which the two fighters know, but it is not yet known to the watchers. Nobody is going to win. The dilemma is how nobody is going to lose. It has early been established that the black boy will hit the white boy on the head with a sound like splitting a melon—but it's the white boy who moves forward, the black boy who moves back. It isn't clear if the white boy, or any of the watchers, perceives the method in this tactic. Each step backward the black boy takes he is closer to home, and nearer to darkness.

In time they cross the cinder-covered yard to the narrow steps going down to the sidewalk. There the fight is delayed while a passing adult, a woman with a baby sitting up in its carriage, tells them to stop acting like children, and asks their names to inform their teachers. The black boy's name is Eustace Beecher. The white boy's name is Emil Hrdlic, or something like that. He's a real saphead, and not at all certain how it is spelled. When the woman leaves, they return to their fighting and go along the fronts of darkened houses. Dogs bark. Little dogs, especially, enjoy a good fight.

The black boy has changed his style of fighting so that his bleeding nose doesn't drip on his shirt. The white boy has switched around to give his cramped, cocked arm a rest. The black boy picks up support from the fact that he doesn't take advantage of this situation. One reason might be that his left eye is almost closed. When he stops to draw a shirtsleeve across his face, the white boy does not leap forward and strike him. It's a good fight. They have learned what they can do and what they can't do.

At the corner lit up by the bug-filled streetlamp they lose about half of their seven spectators. It's getting late and dark. You can smell the bread baking on the bakery draft. The light is better for the fighters now than the watchers, who see the two figures only in profile. It's not so easy anymore to see which one is black and which one is white. Sometimes the black boy, out of habit, takes a step backward, then has to hop forward to his proper position. The hand he thrusts out before him is limp at the wrist, as if he had just dropped something unpleasant. The white boy's shirt, once blue in color, shines like a slicker on his sweaty back. The untied laces of his shoes are broken from the way he is always stepping on them. He is the first to turn his head and check the time on the bakery clock.

Behind the black boy the street enters the Negro section. Down there, for two long blocks, there is no light. A gas streetlamp can be seen far at the end, the halo around it swimming with insects. One of the two remaining fight watchers whistles shrilly, then enters the bakery to buy penny candy. There's a gum-ball machine that sometimes returns your penny, but it takes time, and you have to shake it.

The one spectator left to watch this fight stands revealed in the glow of the bakery window. One pocket is weighted with marbles; the buckles of his britches are below his knees. He watches the fighters edge into the darkness where the white shirt of the black boy is like an object levitated at a séance. Nothing else can be seen. Black boy and white boy are swallowed up. For a moment one can hear the shuffling feet of the white boy; then that, too, dissolves into darkness. The street is a tunnel with a lantern gleaming far at its end. The last fight-watcher stands as if paralyzed until the rumble of a passing car can be felt through the soles of his shoes, tingling the blood in his feet. Behind him the glow of the sunset reddens the sky. He goes toward it on the run, a racket of marbles, his eyes fixed on the FORD sign beyond the school building, where there is a hollow with a shack used by ice skaters under which he can crawl and peer out like a cat. When the streetlights cast more light he will go home.

Somewhere, still running, there is a white boy who saw all of this and will swear to it; otherwise, nothing of what he saw remains. The Negro section, the bakery on the corner, the red-brick school with one second-floor window (the one that opens out on the fire escape) outlined by the chalk dust where they slapped the erasers— all of that is gone, the earth leveled and displaced to accommodate the ramps of the new freeway. The cloverleaf approaches look great from the air. It saves the driving time of those headed east or west. Omaha is no longer the gateway to the West, but the plains remain, according to one traveler, a place where his wife still sleeps in the seat while he drives through the night.

1970

Green Grass, Blue Sky,
White House

As I sit here, Floyd's mother mows the lawn. The whine of the mower can be heard above the noise of her grandchildren at their horseplay. If I close my eyes the sounds are like those we see in comic strips, WHAM! BAM! POWIE!, rising like balloons, or exploding like firecrackers. All in fun, of course. They are healthy, growing animals and have to work off their energies somehow. Why not with the mower? Mrs. Collins likes to mow her own lawn. Any day but Sunday, either Franklin DeSpain, or Lyle, or even Melanie, would pop up from somewhere and do it for her, but Reuben De-

Spain insists that his children keep the Sabbath holy. The Lord rested, and so do the DeSpains.

A farm girl to begin with, Mrs. Collins likes to get her hands on a machine that works and work it. The blades spin free when she nears a tree and uses short, choppy strokes. The whine of the mower makes its way around the house, and on the long run at the back it is almost gone. It stops when twigs from the elms catch between the blades. I can tell she likes to work around the tree trunks where the short, hard strokes set the blades to whirring. That's a sound from my boyhood. The whirring blades of a mower pushed by somebody else. I would wait for the thump as it hit the house at the end of its run. People in this country once might have been divided into those who knew that sound and those who didn't; those who liked it and those it made almost sick. All summer long, freshly cut lawn grass weighted the cuffs of my father's pants.

One of Franklin DeSpain's boys walks by with a skateboard he carries around looking for sidewalks. Not all the streets in Ordway have them. The lawns slope down to bleed into the weeds, and the weeds into the crumbling blacktop. Most of the walks in town are of brick heaved into waves and troughs by tree roots. The only walking people do is from the door at the back of the house to the car parked in the drive.

The town of Ordway, in Missouri, is one where no line is drawn between what is rural and what is urban. A cow is tethered in the lot facing the square, where the sidewalk bristles with parking meters. I've seen no pigs, but the older residents, like Floyd's mother, keep a goat, or a cow, or a few fenced chickens. Everything is here to make the good life possible. Mrs. Collins at one point gave up the chickens but Mr. Collins missed their cackling. The silence disturbed his rest in the morning. If she forgets to collect the eggs, they soon have an old hen with a fresh batch of chicks. Almost an acre of lawn surrounds the house, and there is sometimes snow in the yard till Easter, the first spears of spring grass pale as winter wheat. At the back it's hard to tell where the lawn ends and the fields begin.

One thing I have learned is that small-town people have a pallor you can seldom find in the city. If they roll up a sleeve, or tuck up a pants leg, the bit of skin that shows is white as a flour sack. Mrs. Collins wears a pair of Floyd's unlaced tennis sneakers on her bare feet. His sweaters also fit her. Her overalls, however, once belonged to Mr. Collins, and the seat and knees are patched with pieces of quilting. That makes for more comfort when she kneels to weed, and less dampness when she sits to cut greens. A faded gingham sunbonnet sits back on her head to let the sun warm her face.

In the fall the yard is so bright with leaves Mrs. Collins tells me it's almost painful to look at. They have to pull the shades at the windows to sleep at night. Both a fact of that sort or a death in the family Mrs. Collins reports with an appealing smile. If my eyes are on her face I often miss the gist of what she is saying. Her expression remains the same: a beaming smile, an affable, open good nature. If I hear her laughing, it is usually at herself. This can be disconcerting when it signals something is wrong. She laughed, her daughter tells me, when she fell and broke her hip. Of Scotch descent, with a long Quaker family background, Mrs. Collins believes "the slings and arrows of misfortunes," as she says, are as much to be experienced as anything else. Nothing has diminished her appetite for life.

The Collins house is *substantial,* as my father would have said, with a run-around porch that is tilted like a ship's deck, the spacious lawn shaded by sycamores and elms. There's a cleared spot at the back, hard as blacktop, where the trash and the leaves are burned. The two-board gap in the fence indicates a shortcut that connects the Collins house with the one across the alley. Her daughter Ruth lives there, but Ruth's three teen-age boys spend most of their time in the Collins kitchen, or rough-housing at the back of the yard. A trough is worn into the yard where a tire swings from the limb of an elm.

The Collins kitchen is big, and uncluttered with modern conveniences. Mrs. Collins makes my toast under the flame in the oven, then scrapes the char off at the sink. She does not believe in anything, as she says, "that you have to plug in." The crackle of her long hair, worn in a loose bun at her neck, is her daily assurance that her health is in order and her battery is charged. In the house she wears a simple gray frock with touches of faded lace at the wrists and throat. I've no idea if she knows how much it does for her corn-yellow hair. She prefers to stand, rather than sit, her hip inclined on the stove rail, or the sink, with one of her brown freckled hands holding a loose wad of her apron, cupped in her palm. She tests heat and flavor with her fingers, spits on the skillet before making hotcakes. Into the first pot of percolator coffee she puts a pinch of salt and one fresh eggshell, preferably white. I'm told that the house swarmed with cats until her daughter Ruth married and took most of them with her. Mrs. Collins says, "I don't mind having pets, but I don't like the pets having people," meaning Mr. Collins and his old dog Ruby, now dead three years. Every day in his life, which proved to be a long one, Ruby would walk Mr. Collins to the railroad crossing, look up and down in both directions, then lead him across if it was safe. When Mr. Collins stopped making the walk, Ruby went under the house porch and refused to come out. It was the end of the run for both Ruby and the St. Louis & Troy.

Although it is fifteen years since a train entered Ordway, Mr. Collins still wears the striped overalls preferred by trainmen, and one of the high-crowned, long-billed brakeman's hats. This he leaves on his head until Mrs. Collins says, "Papa, your cap." All members of the family speak of him as Papa, but not often to his face. His skin is smooth, as if dampened and then stretched on his skull. The abundance of his hair gives the impression that his head is not fully developed, or with time has shrunk. His pale blue eyes have a focus just beyond the object of his attention. Before speaking he nervously fingers the bill of his cap. The two subjects Mr. Collins never loses sight of are Norman Thomas and the old dog Ruby. A picture of Ruby, a gourd-shaped little terrier with his head almost swallowed by his thickening neck, is among the family portraits on the sewing machine. More recent snapshots, featuring the grandchildren, Waldo, Luther, and Clarence, are on the piano. Waldo and Luther take after their father, a huge, affable man in the road-construction business. The younger boy, Clarence, is small-boned like his mother, but almost six feet tall. He has grown too fast, and his movements are those of a boy on stilts. The boys like to roughhouse and can usually be heard clopping up and down the stairs of the Collins house, chased by Clarence, or mawling like dogs at the back of the yard. Waldo has picked up such lingo as "Sock it to me!" supplemented with cries of "Wham! Bam! Powie!" The trouble starts when Clarence, wearing one of Melanie's aprons, helps her wash and dry the dishes.

It is a point of pride with Mrs. Collins that she has no keys; the house is never locked. Back in the Depression, when they took in roomers, the keys disappeared in the pockets of strangers, and Mrs. Collins has never troubled to replace them. Mr. Collins pads through my room, while I sleep, because it has always been his way to the bathroom. If he took another route, strange to his habits, he might easily stumble or bump into something. To close a door so that it clicks is to imply that you have something to hide. It has been years since the bathroom door actually latched shut. If it is closed, the draft nudges it open. During the night the light provides a beacon, and the drip in the tub is like the tick of a clock. Unless the bathroom door stands open wide, it is safe to assume there is someone behind it. Most members of the family make a characteristic sound when steps approach. Mrs. Collins hums, Melanie turns on a faucet in the bowl and lets it run. Mr. Collins, however, is absolutely silent. He sits dreaming on the stool, his brown hands on his white knees, his gaze on the leaf-clogged gutters of the porch visible from the bathroom window. An intruder need not disturb him. The boys shower while he sits there. Privacy can be had by going up one floor and using the small water closet, but the flush of the water when the chain is pulled seems designed to clean out miles of plumbing, and burps in all the sinks.

If this were not Sunday, or if the grass had been mowed, Mrs. Collins would be seated in the porch rocker. It is of wood, the rungs turned by hand, the cane seat so new it resembles plastic. Layers of green and brown paint are visible where Mrs. Collins grips the chair arms. She takes a strong grip when she rocks, as if she feared the chair might take off. The spreading legs are reinforced with baling wire still fuzzy with the hair of the Collins cats. They used to retire there to get away from Ruby, and one of the toms had his tail amputated. Never again did he set foot on the Collins porch.

At one time as many as eight or ten children ran in and out of the house, and sagged the rails of the porches. The chain swing had to be taken down to keep them from wearing a hole in the clapboards. They *had* to rock it sideways, or swing it so high the whole house leaned one way, then the other. The hooks for the swing are still there in the ceiling, but who would swing if they put it back up? Not the new generation. The porch stoop used to sag with the DeSpain children, who were too polite to use the hammock. They were noisy, but they had breeding and refused to do a lick of work on Sunday. Mr. Collins would torment them by offering them money to run down and buy him his White Owl cigar. The other days of the week they had to offer to do it for nothing. For every biscuit that was eaten at the Collins table, two biscuits went out the door with Rosemary DeSpain, Reuben's wife, along with what she loosely defined as "leftovers." She in turn donated her coffee stamps during the war, when Mr. Collins began to suffer his withdrawal headaches. He was accustomed to eight strong cups a day, and that was what he got. Sunday being the day of rest, the DeSpains liked to spend it where they could watch other people work. Rosemary is gone now, but Mrs. Collins tells me she got up early to sit in the Collins kitchen, watching Ruth and Mrs. Collins prepare the Sunday meal. In case she ever had to do it, she wanted to be sure she knew how it was done.

Reuben DeSpain tells me that his wife was black and blue as a new stovepipe, but their children and grandchildren are best described as "golden oak." DeSpain claims that it comes from his French and Castilian ancestry. The boys have their father's light copper tan, but Melanie is so pale out-of-town people take her for an Italian, like Sophia Loren. She has Sophia's big, halfpopped eyes and wide, full mouth. Mrs. Collins likes to tell how Floyd would ask her why his own tan peeled and Melanie's didn't. Unless she smiles, or talks, her impassive expression appears to be sullen. Melanie is inclined to be accident-prone, and wears Band-Aids on her fingers and arms for stove burns. The burn soon heals, but the print of the adhesive leaves a visible pattern. Mrs. Collins says to her, "Melanie, that stove bite you again?" Melanie's chores are to cook, tidy up, make the beds, and hand-wash Floyd's dress shirts in case he dirties any. She leaves the ironing board standing, blocking the pantry, to show that a woman's work is never done. She smokes Camels as she works, dropping the ashes on the ironing and between the sheets.

"One day you're going to burn this house down," Mrs. Collins says, and both women laugh. Melanie leaves the butts resting on the ashtrays, the edges of the bureaus, windowsills, and cereal cartons, or they slow-burn holes in the oilcloth or char a hole in the plastic soap dishes, or burn down till they tilt off something and drop to the floor. When Melanie laughs she turns her back and you see the top of her head rather than the roof of her mouth. She takes shame in her dark laughter, and wipes it off her mouth before she turns to face me. Around the house, as a dust cap, she wears a shower hat in which she stores her matches and pack of Camels. Thinking up things to keep Melanie "busy" is one of Mrs. Collins' endless chores. While Melanie wanders around tidying up, Mrs. Collins prepares for her the well-balanced lunch she never gets at home. Left to herself Melanie will eat nothing but creamed canned corn and chipped beef in a white sauce. She loves diet cola spiked with a spoonful of chocolate syrup. The two women eat together, discussing samples of cloth Mrs. Collins receives from a store in Chicago. She has in mind a dress for herself and a new winter coat for Melanie.

One of Floyd's chores, when he was at home, was to pick up Melanie in the morning and get her home to make her father's supper in the evening. On arriving, Melanie calls out, "Here I am, Mrs. Collins," and waits until she is told what to do. They both have a cup of coffee while they plan her day's work.

"What'll I do now?" is perhaps the one thing that Mrs. Collins hears the most. Finding work to do for Franklin, Lyle, and Melanie gets Mrs. Collins up early and often keeps her awake. "Before I ever make a move," Mrs. Collins tells me, "the first thing I think of is Franklin and Lyle." They don't like to be idle, but they like her to tell them what to do. Mrs. Collins has never gone to some of the places she would like to, because the DeSpains take so much looking after. Especially Reuben, who can't stand to be idle now his wife is dead. This being Sunday, however, he is willing to sit in front of the barn under a new painted sign that reads:

REUBEN DESPAIN
I buy junk and sell antiques

He doesn't buy junk, of course, he gets it all free, but one of his clients thought the remark would make a good sign. DeSpain came to Ordway in the early years of the Depression, when some of the whites, as well as the "coloreds," took their pay in milk and eggs and leftovers. His children wore the clothes the Collins children grew out of. He never complained. For twenty-five years he walked a horse and wagon—the horse wearing a bonnet to ward off sunstroke—up one street and down the other collecting whatever people had to throw away, or believed they had worn out. After the war it began to add up. The software, so called, Rosemary DeSpain cleaned up and sold once a year in the Methodist basement; the hardware Reuben DeSpain stowed away in the Collins barn. The government didn't want it, you couldn't eat it, or sell it, and it wouldn't burn. To make room for such stuff one of the Collins cars had to sit out in the yard, splattered with bird droppings, or in the freezing winter weather over one of the grease pits in the Collins service station. The other car, a Model T Ford with a brass radiator and a California top, had become so old it belonged in the barn as part of the junk. It had never actually been *given* to Reuben DeSpain but, as Floyd liked to say, it had been *ceded* to him. It had been *thought* to be junk, and if it was junk it belonged to DeSpain. A gentleman in Des Moines has an option on the car, and pays five dollars a month for DeSpain to store it for him. He doesn't seem to mind that the price of the car goes up and up. Two or three times a year a woman from St. Louis comes over in her station wagon for DeSpain's old bottles, beaded lampshades, wall and mantel clocks, oil lamps, and old records. A Philadelphia firm that makes stoves will buy anything good DeSpain lays a hand on, including the old Mayflower coke burner he warms his house with over the winter. It has a "sold" tag on it, but he is free to use it while he is still around. There's more people than DeSpain can keep track of to collect the buttons he snips off old clothes. Mrs. Collins has explained, and DeSpain has grasped, that as money gets cheaper his junk gets dearer. He lets it sit. DeSpain won't sell his records or his clocks to people who impress him as careless in such matters. Clocks run for him. Once off the premises they stop. There's an account at the bank for Reuben DeSpain and family that will pass on to his heirs if they can bother to be troubled. Money is something they don't understand, and have always left to Floyd. Besides Melanie, Franklin, and Lyle, there are Franklin's three children. In the mid-fifties Franklin, a year older than Lyle, took fifty dollars from the bank and went to Chicago where he planned a new start. He left in June and was back in October. A few years later Lyle went to St. Louis, where he enrolled in a Peace Corps program. He learned to type, and returned with a machine on which he still owed thirty-eight dollars. Both boys were noncommittal, but according to Mrs. Collins they were shocked by people's behavior. They were also homesick, and tired of people who called light-colored boys black.

Finding work for them to do was a strain for Mrs. Collins until Floyd thought of installing a car wash at the back of the service station. Running the station is a family enterprise, and all members of the family contribute to it. When Floyd was at home, he ran it; and Ruth's husband runs it in the slack season for road work; and there is always Mrs. Collins, or one of Ruth's boys, to help at the pumps on a busy weekend. The car wash occupies space once used for parking, and does a good business with college boys from Mason City. Franklin and Lyle are good workers, but they seem to lack initiative. They work better when Mrs. Collins is around, and they like her to handle the accounts. Franklin's two eldest boys are very good with a wax job, but it doesn't help matters that one has the name *Floyd*. This seemed very touching when Franklin's son was born, but it led to nothing but complications. When someone hollered "Floyd," both Floyds answered. The result was that Floyd Collins would seldom answer when his name was called. He didn't mean to be rude, or insist on *Mr.* Collins, but what could he do?

From where I am seated I can't see but I can hear the hiss and spray of steam at the car wash, and the sound of the gong as a car pulls into the station. Until just recently Reuben DeSpain took care of such things as the tires, windshields, etc., but all that stooping and bending didn't help his back any, and his right arm, especially his "windshield elbow," seemed to get worse. All he had to do was pick up a rag and he would feel the twinge of pain. Mrs. Collins thought he'd better just sit and take it easy, before it got so he couldn't use his arm to eat with. There's nothing harder for Reuben to do than just sit, but that's now what he does. His platform rocker, covered with plum-colored velvet once popular on tram seats, sits under a beach umbrella in the dappled shade at the front of the barn. The arms are too low, the back is too high, and the angle is all wrong for comfort, but DeSpain has never lost his taste for elegance. His ancestors, by published account, were influential pirates and patrons of the arts. He has the nose, forehead, and melancholy eyes of the clergy painted by El Greco. He also has the style. If DeSpain is asked if he has something or other, he will reply, "I shall endeavor to ascertain it," then go and look. For seven years he was one of the servants close to Governor Huey Long. He considers the Governor one of the country's great men. Five weeks following the assassination, DeSpain and his family, on their way to Chicago, were towed into Ordway by a Mason City milkman. The car had broken down. It proved to be an Essex, of a year and a model for which parts were no longer available. Mr. Collins let them camp in the railroad station where they could use the lavatories and the drinking fountain, while Reuben DeSpain considered his next move. That proved to be into the barn behind the Collins house. In a few weeks' time Mrs. Collins hardly knew how she had ever got along without him. "Ma'am," he said, "all Reuben DeSpain aims to do is please."

Some of the younger generation think of DeSpain as a swami, thanks to his remarkable elegance of speech. He need say no more than "Consider the lilies—" to gather a group of teen-age loafers around him. On warm sultry days, between his neck and his collar he slips a clean white kerchief scented with insect repellent. He claims it keeps him free of pests while he naps. He wears a carpenter's apron with the big nail pockets full of un-sorted parking-meter pennies. He gets them from the Ordway police department. Sorting them carefully by hand, he turns up the coins he sells to a collector in Independence. Real copper pennies are so close to De-Spain's color you feel they got it from the rubbing he gives them to bring out the dates.

On weekdays you can see Franklin or Lyle seated at the barn door tinkering with something that doesn't work. There is never an end. Just putting up the house screens and taking them down takes two or three weeks. Reuben DeSpain sits in his chair brushing off the rust with a whisk broom, his gesture that of a railroad porter dusting the lapels of Huey Long. In the winter he sits inside the barn and mends the holes. Mrs. Collins likes to feed her own chickens and collect the eggs (when there are any), but without Lyle around to milk her, the cow, Bessie, won't give her milk. In the spring the sheds need to be fumigated and the fourteen trees on the lot pruned and sprayed. In the dry spells everything has to be watered, which means dragging the hoses from faucet to faucet, the pressure sometimes getting so low it won't operate the sprinkler: Franklin's boys will have to water the tomato plants with the watering can. Both Franklin and Lyle dislike spray nozzles and prefer to stand, using their thumbs, soaking up the water with their shoes and pants legs. When a toilet bowl in the house is flushed, the pressure drops and the outside water goes off.

Inside the house the drains get clogged and water stands for days in the second-floor tub. Periodically roots close the lines to the cesspool although the nearest tree is forty-eight feet: what a root will do in its search for water defies belief. The lawn grass grows so thick right over the cesspool Mrs. Collins has to run at it with the mower, but she will not cut or use table greens from that part of the yard. Melanie has been warned not to do it, either, but somehow she forgets.

I've noticed the whole house shakes when the boys come clopping down the stairs. The pigeons kept by a neighbor, in a roost on his roof, go up on the sky like a cloud of smoke. There's always one that doesn't seem to get the swing of it, his wings flapping like a loose fan belt. Off where I can't see them, but I can hear them, Waldo and Luther are starting their horseplay. They go through the kitchen, slamming the screen, then clop around the house like cantering horses. Waldo is the one who strips the leaves off the lilac bushes as he makes the turns. These daily runs have not worn away the grass, but they have firmed it down so that it has a different color and texture, like the flattened wale of corduroy or the plush seat of a chair. Waldo is always first, a step or two ahead of Luther, and Clarence trails along like a caboose. If Luther stops suddenly, dropping to his knees, Clarence will stumble over him as if he were a bench. He never seems to learn. The green smears of grass will not wash off his elbows and bony knees. They all make about two hooting circles of the house, then Waldo heads for the clearing at the back. Where the tire swing dangles from the limb of an elm, he grasps the rope to keep from collapsing. He can't seem to stop laughing. Luther is so winded he trips on his own feet, and sprawls out on his face. He lies there giggling as if he were being tickled to death. Clarence comes along so many moments later he seems part of another scene. I first thought he had tired and run down, like a spring-wound toy. But he had merely paused to pick up a length of clothesline. He straddles Luther and flails at him with the rope—but it's too long. He can't bring it around with the proper snap. Waldo is so winded he can hardly breathe, but he hoarsely yells, "Sock it to 'im! Sock it to 'im!" Clarence tries to. The sound is that of someone beating a carpet with a small switch. Luther will not stop giggling, and Clarence cries, "I'm going to kill you! You hear me?" Waldo is still hooting, but he has sagged to drape his arms around the tire. In that position Clarence is able to flail him as if he were a slave clamped in the stocks or tied to a whipping post.

From behind the house Mrs. Collins appears holding aloft one of her leather-palmed cotton work gloves. She wags it as she comes, with loping, silent strides, to where Clarence towers over Waldo. No word is spoken. Waldo and Luther are hooting, but it appears to be a scene on silent film. All my life, or so it seems, I have watched roughhousing boys interrupted in their play by the long arm of Tom Sawyer's Aunt Polly. With a practiced gesture she grips Clarence, wheels him about, and slaps him (POWIE!) with the glove. He straightens to stand like a machine with the power switched off. From his dangling hand she takes the rope and shortens it to give him a slap across the buttocks. With a hoot, he takes off. In an instant he is followed by Waldo, who lunges to avoid the swipe she gives him. Luther is last; he goes off howling with a gleeful shriek. I hear the screen door to the kitchen open and slam, and then the clop of their feet on the front-hall stairs. The house rocks. I feel it like an earth tremor in the boards of the porch. After a bout of such horseplay all three boys like to take long showers with their clothes on, then come down and sit in the lawn swing to dry off.

Mrs. Collins stands, her face to the sky, watching the whirring flight of the neighbor's pigeons. The disturbance has flushed her face with color; she idly slaps the shortened length of rope on her thigh. "My, how we all miss Floyd!" she says, coming toward me, and her smile is that of a priestess at the close of a ceremony. She feels better, the boys feel better, and she would like to assure me I should feel better. What is a little violence in the larger ceremony of innocence? She turns a gaze toward Mr. Collins, who stands in the garden, leaning on a hand plow. His straw hat is wider than his shoulders, and the wide limp brim rests on his ears. He looks more like a boy daydreaming at his chores than an old man resting. Nor does he move from his reverie until he hears the whirring blades of the mower.

On my drive down from Chicago (I was given ten days to look into the Collins case) I stopped in St. Louis for a talk with Floyd. They're holding him there, as we say, for observation. He's a good-looking, rustically hand-some boy with his mother's jaw and prominent features. I see they suit a man's face better than they do hers. He has the casual, cool manner of most young people, and lets his hair grow long at the back. While we talked he preferred to sit on the floor with his knees drawn up. Off and on he toyed with a piece of cellophane from his pack of Camel cigarettes, blowing on it softly as he held it pressed, like a blade of grass, between his thumbs. The sound emitted is high and shrill, like a trapped insect or a fingernail on glass. I once made such a sound, or tried to, blowing through a dandelion stem.

To the President of the United States Floyd Collins wrote: *I am obliged to inform you your life is threatened. I am a reasonable man. It is reason that compels me to take this action. I propose to take your one life to spare the tens of thousands of innocent men, women, and children. Please stop this war or accept the consequences.*

I liked the "please." It showed his responsible Quaker

breeding and will also help to commute his sentence, since no shot was fired. During my stay in Ordway, Mrs. Collins has treated me like "one of the family," and that is how I feel. One of the family. Some, if not all, of the emotions Floyd Collins has felt. I see a cow grazing, Reuben DeSpain napping, a blue sky towers above me and green grass surrounds me, and inside the white house I hear boys at their horseplay, training to be men.

"I raised Floyd to believe anything is possible," Mrs. Collins says. As it is, of course. Here in Ordway anything is possible. Not necessarily what Mrs. Collins has in mind, or Floyd has in mind, or even the town of Ordway has in mind, but what a dream of the good life, and reasonable men, make inevitable.

1969

Magic

Robert could see Father in the front seat, steering. He could see Mother and the lover in the back seat, sitting. They came around the lake past the Japanese lanterns and Mrs. Van Zant's idea of a birthday party. The car stopped and Father got out and opened the door for Mother. Mother got out and pulled her dress down. She leaned back in and said, "Here we are—here we are, lover!"

"I object to your sentimentality," said Father.

"Here we are, lover," Mother said, and pulled him out of the car. His arms stuck out of the sleeves of his coat. One pocket of his pants was pulled inside out. Robert wanted to see the bump on his head but he had on his hat. "Here we are," Mother said, and turned him to look at Robert.

"This is Mr. Brady, son," said Father.

"I told you," Mother said, "Callie's boyfriend."

"Where's Callie?" said Robert.

"Callie's got her lungs full of water, baby. She's where they'll dry her out."

"He's dried out?" asked Robert. He didn't look it. There was a line around his hat where the water had stopped. Under the hat, where he had the bump, Mother said his head was shaved. "Why'd she hit him?"

"She didn't hit him, baby. He fell on it. When they fell out of the boat, he fell on it."

"A likely story," Father said. "Is that Emily?"

Robert's sister Emily stood in the door holding one of Robert's rabbits and wearing both of Callie's slippers.

"Go put your clothes on!" Father said.

"My God, why?" cried Mother. "She's cute as cotton. Why would anybody put some lousy clothes on it?"

"Don't shout!" shouted Father.

To the lover Emily said, "Did you ever hug a rabbit?"

"He doesn't want to hug a rabbit," Father said, "or see little girls with all their clothes off."

"Why not?" Mother said.

"Mr. Brady is not well," said Father. "When he fell from the boat he bumped his head and was injured."

"Where does he hurt?" said Robert.

"In his heart, baby."

"Mr. Brady has lost his memory," said Father.

"What a wonderful way to be," said Mother.

"How does he do it?" asked Robert.

Father said, "You don't *do* it. It just happens. You forget to feed your rabbits. He has forgotten his name."

"Isn't he wonderful?" Mother said. She took his hand. "You must be starving!"

"They said he had just eaten," said Father. "Where you going to put him?"

"Did Callie lose her memory, too?" asked Robert.

Mother said, "No such luck, baby—"

"She has some water in her lungs," said Father, "but she didn't lose her memory. She said she wanted you in bed."

To Emily, Mother said, "Is that the *same* rabbit? My God, if I'm not sick of rabbits."

"Can't they dress themselves without her?" Father said. "Put down that rabbit, will you? Go put some clothes on."

"Isn't she cute as cotton?" Mother said to Mr. Brady. Emily put down the rabbit and showed her funny belly button. Robert's button went in, but Emily's button went out.

"Are you going to speak to her about that?" said Father.

"Show lover your sleeping doll, pet," said Mother.

Emily rolled her eyes back so only the whites showed. Robert called it playing dead.

"I'll show him up," Father said. "Where you putting him?"

"Callie's room!" they both cried.

To Mr. Brady, Mother said, "You like a nap? You take a nap. You take a nice nap, then we have dinner."

Father whinnied. "If Callie's not here, who's going to prepare it?"

Mother hadn't thought about it. She stood thinking, fingering the pins in her golden hair.

"We could eat pizzas!" cried Robert. "Pisa's Pizzas!"

Emily clapped her hands.

"You don't seem to grasp the situation," said Father. "You have a man on your hands. You have a legal situation."

"I hope so," said Mother.

"It's your picnic—" began Father.

"Picnic! Picnic!" Emily cried.

Father rubbed his palms together. "I'll show him up. You dress the children. You like to use the washroom, Mr. Brady?" Father led him down the hall.

Their mother took off the green hat and felt for the pins in her golden hair. She took them out like clothespins, held them in her mouth, while she raised her arms and let the fan cool beneath them. Through the open French doors she could see across the lake to Mrs. Van Zant's lawn and all the Japanese lanterns. Mrs. Van Zant lay in the hammock on the porch with her beach hat on her face. Mother gave Emily her hairpins, then threw back her head so the hair hung down like Lady Godiva's. When she shook her head more hairpins dropped on the polar bear rug. These pins were for Robert. He picked them up and made a tight fistful of them.

"What was I going to say, pet?" Mother said.

"Where's Callie," said Emily.

"In the hospital, baby. She's in Mr. Brady's head. That's why it hurts him."

"He's got no memory?" said Robert.

"Who needs it, baby. Give Mother her pins." His mother sat on the stool between the three mirrors with her long golden hair parted in the middle, fanned out on her front. "Your mother is Lady Godiva," she said.

"Lady Godiva my lawnmower!" said Father. He came through the French doors with a drink and took a seat on the bed.

"You like horses, baby?" Mother said to Robert. "She was the one on the horse."

"Can you picture your mother on a horse?" said Father. "Ho-ho-ho," he laughed.

111

"Tell your father he's no lover," said Mother.

"Tell your mother you could all have done worse," said Father. "Her looks, my brains."

"I'm not sure he understands her," said Mother. "You think he thinks she meant to hit him?"

Father said, "Just so she didn't lose any more than he did."

"She won't like it," said Mother. "She likes to make her own bed and eat her own food. Did you see it? White fish, white sauce, white potatoes, white napkins. I thought I'd puke."

"In my opinion," said Father, "he jumped out of that boat. He tried to drown himself."

"That's love for you," Mother said. "Your father wouldn't understand."

"It's a miracle he *didn't* drown," said Father.

"See how your father sits and stares," said Mother.

"Ppp-shawww, I'm too old for that stuff," said Father.

"God kill me I should ever admit it!" said Mother.

"What I came in to say, was—" Father said, "I'm washing my hands of the whole business."

"You're always washing your hands," Mother said.

"It's no picnic," Father said. "You get a man in the house and the first thing you know you can't get him out."

"No such luck," Mother said.

"I'm warning you—" Father said.

"Tell your father he can go wash his hands!" Mother shouted.

"Eva—" Father said, "there is no need to shout."

"It's this damn house," Mother said. "Twenty-eight rooms and two babies. An old man, and two pretty babies."

"All right," said Father, "have your stroke."

"When I do—" Mother said, "I want someone here

112

with me. I won't have a stroke and be cooped up here alone."

"Eva—" Father said, "that will be enough."

Mother let her long hair slip from her lap and stared at her front face in the mirror. Her mouth was open, and the new bridge was going up and down. She took the bridge out of her mouth and felt along the inside of her mouth with her finger. She spread her mouth wide with her fingers to see if she could see something.

"If you just keep it up," Father said, "you're going to have a little something—"

"Where's my baby?" Mother turned to look for Emily. She was sitting on the head of the polar bear feeding fern leaves to the rabbit. "If you do that he'll make beebees," Mother said. "You want him to go around the house making beebees?"

"It's not a him," said Robert, "it's a her."

"You have to shout?" shouted Father. "We're sitting right here."

"That's why *I* have to shout!" shouted Mother.

"Don't pick her up," Father said, "put her down. It's picking her up that makes beebees. If you don't want beebees pick her up by the ears."

Emily picks her up by the ears, then puts her down.

"I swear to God you're all crazy," Mother said. "Who could ever like that?"

Father takes his drink from the floor and holds it out toward Robert. There is a fly in it. "You see that?" Robert saw it. "What is it?"

"A fly," said Robert.

"Don't let him fool you, baby."

"Son—" said Father, "what kind of fly is it?"

"Are you crazy?" said Mother.

"Not so fast," said Father, "what kind of fly is it?"

"A drownded fly," said Robert.

"A drowned fly," said Father.

"Why should he look at a drowned fly?" said Mother.

Father didn't answer. He held the glass close to his face and blew on the fly as if to cool it. It rocked on the water but nothing happened.

"You would agree the fly is drowned?" his father asked.

"Don't agree to anything, baby."

"I'm going to hold this fly under water," said Father, "while you go and bring your father a saucer and a saltcellar."

"Don't you do it," said Mother.

"Obey your father," said Father.

Robert put his mother's hairpins in her lap and went back through the club room, the dining room, the game room, through the swinging door into the kitchen. Callie's metal saltcellar sat on the stove, where the heat kept it dry. He sprinkled some on the floor, crunched on it, then carried it back through the house to his father.

"Where's the saucer?" Father said.

"They're not for flies," said Mother. She took the ashtray from her dresser and passed it to Robert. Father used his silver pencil to push the fly to the edge of the glass, then fish it out. A drowned fly. It lay on its back, its wings stuck to the ashtray.

"This fly has been in the water twenty minutes," said Father. "That's a lot longer than your Mr. Brady."

"What did you drown him for?" asked Robert.

"I got the urge," said Father. "Cost me a drink!"

"It's probably a *her*," Mother said. "If it drowns, it's a her."

Father took the blotter from Mother's writing table and used one corner of it to pick up the fly. The drowned fly made a dark wet spot on the blotter. "Mumbo-jumbo, abracadabra—" chanted Father. "Your father will now bring the fly to life!" He put the blotter with the fly on the ashtray, then sprinkled the fly all over with salt. He kept sprinkling until the salt covered the fly like snow.

"My God, what next?" said Mother.

"It is now twenty-one minutes past five," said Father, and held out his watch so Robert could read it.

"Twenty-two minutes," said Robert.

"It was twenty-one when I started," said Father. "It was twenty-two when we had him covered. It takes awhile for the magic to work."

"What magic?"

"Bringing the dead to life," said Father. He took one of Mother's cork-tipped cigarettes, lit it with her lighter, then swallowed the smoke.

"It's not coming out your ears," Emily said.

"That's another trick," said Father, "not this one." He swallowed more smoke, then he held the glowing tip of the cigarette very close to the fly. From where she sat Mother threw her brush at him and it skidded on the floor. "What we need is some light on the subject," said Father, "but more light than that." He looked around the room to the lamp Mother used to make her face brown. "Here we are," said Father, and pulled the lamp over. He held it so the green blotter and the salt were right beneath it. Robert could not see the fly. The brightness of the light made the green look blue. "Feel that!" said Father, and put his face beneath it.

"My God, you look like a turkey gobbler," Mother said.

"When you get my age—" Father began.

"What makes you think I'm going to get your age?" said Mother.

"Well, well—" Father said, "did you see it?"

"What?" said Robert.

"At sixty-two years of age," said Father, "I find my eye

is sharper than yours. You know why?"

"Tell him your mother knows why," said Mother.

"You know why?" Father said. "I have trained myself to look out the corner of my eye. Out of the corner we can detect the slightest movement. With the naked eye we can pick up the twitch of a fly."

"How your father's taste has changed!" cried Mother.

Up through the salt, like the limb of a snowman, appeared the leg of the fly. "Look! Look!" cried Robert.

"Four minutes and twenty seconds," said Father. "Brought him around in less time than it took to drown him." The fly used his long rear legs like poles to clean off the snow. Using his naked eyes just like Father, Robert could see the hairs on the legs, like brushes. He used them like dusting crumbs from the table. He began to wash off his face, like a cat. "Five minutes and forty seconds so far," said Father.

"Does he know who he is?" asked Robert.

"The salt soaked up the water," said Father, and used the silver pencil to tip the fly to his feet. The fly buzzed but didn't fly anywhere. He buzzed like he felt trapped.

"How many times can he do it?" said Robert.

"A good healthy fly," said Father, "can probably come back four or five times."

"Don't he get tired?" Robert said.

"You get tired of anything," Father said, and picked up the fly, dropped him back into the drink. He just lay there, floating on the top. He didn't buzz.

"He's pooped," said Emily.

"Pooped?" said Father. "Where did she hear that?" Mother was looking at her face close to the mirror. Father pushed the fly under the water but he didn't buzz. "No reaction," said Father. He put the glass and the ashtray on Mother's dresser. "He's probably an old fly,"

Father said, "it probably wasn't the first time somebody dunked him."

"What's that?" Mother said. There was a flapping around from the direction of the game room.

"You leave the screen up, son?" Father said. When Robert left the screens up bats flew into the house because it was dark. They had flown so close to Robert the wind of their wings had ruffled his hair. Her golden hair fanned out on her shoulders, Mother went to the hall door and threw it open. The flapping sound stopped.

"Callie!" Mother called, "is that you, Callie?"

"You crazy?" said Father. "Her lungs are full of water. She almost drowned."

"What a lunch!" said Mother. "You ever see anything like it? If I know her she just won't stand it."

There was a wheezing sound, then suddenly music. Through the dark beyond his mother, across the tile-floored room, Robert could see the keys of the piano playing.

"My God, it's him!" said Mother. "It's the lover!"

Father got up from the bed and put the robe with the dragons around her shoulders. He used both hands to lift her hair from inside it. Mother crossed the hall, her robe tassels dragging, to where the cracked green blinds were drawn at the windows. "You poor darling!" she cried, jerking on the blind cords. "How can you see in the dark?" When the blind zipped up Robert could see the lover sitting on the bench at the player piano. His legs pumped. He gripped the sides of the bench so he wouldn't slip off. He wore his hat but his laces were untied and slapped the floor when he pumped.

"Now how'd he get in *there?*" said Father. "How explain that?"

"Go right on pumping," Mother said, "play as long as

you like." She stooped to read the label on the empty roll box. "The 'Barcarole'! Imagine!"

"It's not," said Robert.

"I'd like to have it explained," Father said. "The only closed-up room in the house."

"It's not the 'Barcarole,' " said Robert.

"I know, baby," said Mother. She stood with the empty roll box at the veranda window looking at the lovers' statue in the bird bath. Kissing. One of her orioles splashed them. Across the pond there were cars parked in Mrs. Van Zant's driveway and some of the Japanese lanterns were glowing.

"If only she was here to hear it," Mother said.

Robert said, "She likes it better when you play it backwards."

"If only she was here to see it!" Mother said.

"She's seen it every summer since the war," said Father.

"Oh, no you don't," said Mother. "It's just once you see it."

"Now you see it, now you don't, eh?" said Father. He rubbed his palms together. "When do we eat? Guess I'll go wash my hands."

Mr. Brady, the lover, sat in the covered wicker chair with the paper napkin and the plate in his lap. He wore his hat. He sat looking at Mrs. Van Zant's Japanese lanterns. Out on the pond was a boy in a red inner tube, splashing. Mrs. Van Zant's husband walked around beneath the lanterns, screwing in bulbs.

"All right, all right," Mother said, "but I'm not going to sit on these iron chairs."

"They were your prescription," Father said.

"Not to sit on." Mother spread her napkin on the floor,

118

sat on it. She spread her golden hair on the wicker chair arm.

"Listen to this," Father said, "rain tonight and tomorrow morning. Turning cool late tonight with moderately cool westerly winds." Father wet his finger and put up his hand. "South-westerly," he said.

"Tell your father how we need him," Mother said.

"What about his h-a-t," Father said.

"Don't you think he can s-p-e-l-l?" said Robert.

"Your father never takes anything for granted," Mother said.

"I don't want him forming habits," Father said, "that he's going to find hard to break when he's better."

"I don't think he's hungry," Mother said. "He's thinking about her. I know it."

"Asked him if he'd like a drink. Said he doesn't drink. Asked him if he'd like to smoke. Said he doesn't smoke."

"What's your father mumbling now?"

"A man has to do something—" Father said.

"Which would you rather be—" said Robert, "a rabbit or a hare?"

The lover stood up and spilled his pizza on the floor.

"You can just go and get me another plate," Mother said, and gave the lover the one she was holding. He sat down in the chair and held it in his lap.

"Asked him if he played rummy. He shook his head. Asked him if he played bridge. He shook his head. Suppose you ask him if he can do anything."

"Tell your father how we love him," Mother said.

"I don't care what his field is," Father said, "whether it's stocks and bonds, insurance, or religion. It doesn't matter what it is, a man has to do something. Smoke, drink, play the ponies—he has to do *some*thing."

119

"I never heard a sorrier confession," Mother said. Robert sang—

"Star light, star bright
First star I seen tonight."

"Wouldn't that be *saw?*" Father said.

"SSSShhhhhhh—" said Mother. Across the lake Mrs. Van Zant's loudspeaker was saying something. Mrs. Van Zant's voice came across the water, the people clapped, the drummer beat his drums. More of the Japanese lanterns came on.

"If I don't love the Orient," Mother said.

"You didn't when we were there," Father said. The drummer beat his drums, stopped, and the music played.

"How old is Sylvia now?" Mother said.

"You don't know?" said Father; "or you don't want to know? She's your first one, right? That makes her fifteen this summer."

"I don't know as it matters," Mother said. "The right time is whenever it happens. Heaven knows I was just a little fool when it happened to me."

"I wasn't so smart myself," Father said.

"If my mother had been like some people," Mother said, "she would have locked me in the bedroom, or shipped me off to Boston, or some place like that to a boarding school. But she *knew*—she knew the right time is whenever it happens."

"You talking to me, by chance?" Father said.

"I can honestly say—" Mother said, "I knew what it was the minute I saw her. I knew what it was the minute she came in the house. I knew what it was—I felt the whole business all over again."

"Just what's going on here?" Father said.

Robert jumped up from the steps and ran into the

trees. He ran up and down, back and forth, up and down. He ran around and around the lovers in the bird bath. He stopped running and sang—

> "Beans, beans, the musical fruit
> The more you eat, the more you toot."

"You hear that?" said Father.

"Baby—" Mother said, "we don't sing songs like that."

"I feel it—" Robert said. "I feel it—I feel it!"

"I know, baby," Mother said, "but we don't sing it."

"WHY?" Robert shouted.

"It doesn't show your breeding," Mother said.

Robert stopped jumping up and down and looked across the lake. The Japanese lanterns were waving and the colors were on the water. The music played.

"Time for 'Amos and Andy,' " Father said. The music stopped. A man sang—

> "The moon was all aglow
> And the devil was in your eyes."

"Fifteen is fifteen—" Mother said.

"Robert is eight!" Robert said, and ran up and down, up and down, up and down. The man sang—

> "How deep is the o-shun
> How high is the skyyyy
> How great my de-voshun
> I'll tell you no lie—"

"You ever hear anything like that?" said Father.

"Let it happen when it happens," Mother said, "and whatever else, they can't take it from you." Mother laughed.

Father stood up and walked to the edge of the porch. "You want to make yourself sick? Stop that fool running.

You've just had your supper." Robert ran into the woods and hid. He hid behind the lovers kissing and peeked at the house.

"If you people will excuse me—" Father said, and went inside. He walked down the hardwood floor and turned the radio on, loud.

"You want to be foolish, too?" Mother said.

"No—" Emily said.

"Go be foolish anyhow," Mother said, so Emily ran from the porch and around the sprinkler on the lawn. She ran through the sprinkler and into the trees and splashed her hands in the birdbath, splashing the lovers, splashing Robert in the face. Robert chased her back and forth on the lawn. Robert chased her through the trees, through the garden weeds, and down the cinder path to the pier. He chased her out on the pier and caught her out on the diving board. "Let go of me, you beast!" she said. He let her go.

"What are they doing?" he said.

"They are kissing," she said.

"They are not kissing!" he said.

"They are lovers!" she said, and almost pushed him into the water. Then she ran down the pier and into the grove, around and around the lovers with him behind her, until he caught her and smeared the fresh green slime in her hair. Then they ran around and around the lovers, around the sprinkler, around the veranda, until he caught her and they wrestled in the weeds. They stopped wrestling and lay quiet, listening. The man sang—

> "I walked into an April shower
> I stepped into an open door
> I found a million-dollar baby
> In the five-and-ten-cent stoooore."

"Ba-by—" Mother said. "Oh, ba-by, come and play us something."

"See—" she said, and Robert rolled over, spit in her hair. Then he got up and ran around the house.

The light was on in the music room. From the steps of the veranda he could see the goldfish bowl, the fairy castle, the lamp with the marble base, and the golden braid tassels on the shade. Beyond the lamp he could see part of the lover in the wicker chair.

"You like it fast or you like it slow?" Robert said.

"We like it slow," Mother said, and Robert moved the lever. He held on to the bench and played "Isle of My Golden Dreams." He played it forward, slow, then he played it backward, fast.

"Don't get in your mother's hair, pet—" Mother said.

Robert played "Officer of the Day." He played it forward, fast, then he played it backward, very slow.

"They're playing your song, baby—" Mother said. "Listen to the man singing your song." The man sang—

"You're the cream in my coffee
You're the salt in my stew
You will always be
My ne-cess-ity
I'd be lost without youuuuu."

When the man stopped singing, Robert played "William Tell." He played it backward, very, very slow.

"Oh, Ralph—!" Mother said, "will you speak to your son?" Robert played "It's a Long Way to Tipperary," forward and backward very fast. Mother came in from the veranda and knocked on the folding doors. She tried the folding doors but they wouldn't move.

"You said those doors didn't work," Father said. Father was sitting at his desk with his eyeshade on. He was looking through his magnifying glass at some of his stamps. Mother kicked on the doors. "Now there's no need to get excited—" Father said. Mother went around through the club room and tried the other door.

"Will you unlock this door?" Mother said. Robert played very loud. "Baby—" Mother said, "you know what your mother is going to do?" "Son—" Father said, "you hear what your mother said?"

"You know what Mother's going to do? All right—" she said, "we'll see who likes to be locked in. We'll see who's best at this business of being locked in." Mother went back through the club room, the dining room, and across the hall to her own bedroom door. She opened the door, went in, turned the key in the lock. They could hear her slam the doors to the garden, turn the keys in the locks.

"Now you see what you've done?" Father said. "You know what you are doing to your mother?" Father pounded on the door.

"Tell your father to please go away," Mother said.

"Go to your mother," Father said to Robert. "Your mother is not well. Go to your mother." So he went back through the club room, and the dining room, and knocked at Mother's door.

"It's me, Mother," he said. Mother opened the door and let him in. She kicked her shoes off and went back and lay down on the bed. "You love your mother?"

"Yes, Mother—"

"Yes Mother, yes Mother, yes Mother, yes Mother, yes Mother," his mother said.

"Oh, Eva—?" his father said.

"Your father has the brains of a fish," Mother said.

"I got him stopped," Father said. "You hear? I got him stopped."

"Jabber, jabber, jabber, jabber, jabber—" said Mother.

"He's stopped," Father said. "Why don't you just relax."

"Why don't I have a stroke?" Mother said. "Why don't I have a stroke and let you spoonfeed me?"

"You're distraught," Father said.

"It's a plain simple question," Mother said. "You're a great one for plain simple questions."

"I wash my hands—" Father said, rubbing his palms.

"For the love of mud," said Mother, "go away!"

Father went away. Mother got up from the bed and took a seat on the stool where she had three faces in the mirrors. She put on jar number one and rubbed it in with her fingers. She looked at what she had done and wiped it off with tissue. She put on jar number two, in big thick gobs, and just let it run.

As if he was outside and wanted in Robert said, "Knock, knock, knock."

"Yes, love," said Mother.

Robert put out his fists and said, "Which hand do you take?"

Mother looked at him in one of her mirrors. "You wouldn't fool your mother, baby?"

"Go on, choose," said Robert.

Mother turned on the stool to look at his fists, one green with slime.

"Polliwogs again!"

"You got to choose," he said.

Mother closed her eyes and chose his clean fist. She opened her eyes and looked at what he held in his palm.

"Sugar? Ain't I sweet enough, baby?"

"Why don't you taste it," he said, "it's not sugar."

She held his palm close to her face, sniffed at it, then flicked her tongue at it.

"Salt!" she shouted. "What does your mother want with salt?"

Robert just stood there with the salt in his palm.

At the door Father said, "You two have to shout? I'm going to take him for a walk. Little walk to the village. He's got to do something. The only thing left for him to do is to walk."

Father went away. Through the French doors his mother looked across the pond at the Japanese lanterns and the people dancing. The music came in. Mother said, "That one. What's that?"

"It's not the 'Barcarole,' " said Robert. Mother picked up her brush and stroked it slowly through her golden hair. The electricity crackled. It would lift from her shoulders to be near the brush.

"Do something for your mother, baby." He waited to see what it was. "Go sprinkle it on your father," she said and turned to give him a hug.

1970

In Another Country

Madrid was so dim and sulfurous with smog Carolyn wrote letters to five museum directors, urging them to save the paintings in the Prado while there was still time. Paintings were what Carolyn had come to see, but she actually found it hard with her eyes smarting, her sinuses clogged. Ralph had come to Spain to see Ronda, where they had once planned to honeymoon. Ralph had stumbled on it in Hemingway's bull book as the place a man should go when he bolted with a woman. They had not bolted, but Ralph had always wondered what they had missed, so now they would see. They took a plane to Seville, rented a car, and the same day drove to Arcos de la Frontera, a place hardly on the map but so fabulous Carolyn didn't want to leave. Wasn't it a commonplace that people didn't know when to *stop?* Carolyn did, and she had the premonition that after Arcos anything would be a letdown. They might not have gone on, Carolyn feeling the way she did, if there had been a room for them in Arcos, but the small *parador* was full of English dames from the nineteenth century, one, surely, from the eighteenth century, who received her advice and encouragement through a tuba-shaped ear-horn. A room had been found at a nearby resort, put up in a rush to meet the tourist traffic, the cabins so new the paint seemed sticky, and the sheets on their beds actually proved to be damp.

Carolyn had nearly died, and to keep her from freezing they shared a bed no larger than a cot. Moored at the pier on the artificial lake was a miniature paddle-wheel steamboat, with the word *Mississippi* painted on the prow. It had been too much. Nevertheless, once they were up and had had breakfast, Carolyn had this feeling that Ronda would disappoint them, the view from Arcos being one that nothing could top. Why didn't they just act smart for once and fly to Barcelona and see the Gaudis? Even Ralph liked the Gaudis, or anything you couldn't get into a museum. Why didn't they compromise, Ralph said, and go to Barcelona if Ronda let them down? They might, anyway, if Carolyn's chill turned out to be a cold, which she would rather come down with in Barcelona where they had the name of an American dentist. Whenever they traveled she lost fillings and gained weight.

Their drive to Ronda on a windless spring day was so fabulous it made them both apprehensive. Birds sang, water rippled, the bells on grazing sheep chimed in the distance every time Ralph stopped the car and somewhat frantically took pictures. Was there no end of it? Each time they stopped Carolyn would cry, "Why don't we stop here!" It was a good question, and Ralph explained how the Mormons had faced the same dilemma as they traveled west. Carolyn found the parallel far-fetched but agreed she might feel differently about it if she had been raised in the Midwest, rather than in the East. Ralph was romantic in a way Carolyn wasn't and took the statements of writers personally, following their suggestions to bolt to Ronda, and what to eat and drink. Of course, she liked that about him, up to a point. Over the winter he had read all the books about Spain and tried to persuade her they should travel with a donkey, Spain being the one place in the world a stranger was safe. If it was so gorgeous, Carolyn asked him, why had his great Mr. Hemingstein left it? Ralph thought it had something to do with their civil war. In a gas station on the outskirts of Cordoba the gas attendant had thrown his arms around Ralph, and given him a big hug. He had confused him with some American he had known in the war. It had been difficult for Ralph to persuade him to accept money for the gas. Loyalties of that sort were very touching, and at the same time disturbing. If there had been a war to go to Ralph would have been tempted to enlist.

This morning the slopes of the mountains were green right up to where the granite shimmered like a sunning lizard. In everything Ralph saw, there was some Hemingway. Admittedly, the bottle of wine he had drunk the most of also helped. Carolyn was more enchanted by the white-washed villas in the patterned rows of olive trees. But Carolyn was a realist. She knew what they were like inside. While they sat eating lunch, a man with his ox plowed a jagged furrow maybe forty yards long, frequently pausing to glance at the sky, his own shadow, or nothing at all. Waiting for him to reach the end of the row was a strain for Ralph. He was too much of a Peace

Corps pilgrim at heart to watch a man kill time like that. If he was going to plow, let him plow and get on with it. One of Ralph's forebears combined spring plowing with memorizing passages from the Bible, which replenished the stories he would tell his family all winter. The Bible he had carried in his pocket was one of Ralph's treasured possessions. Here in this earthly paradise the man seemed lower on the scale than the grazing sheep, with their tinkling bells, or the hog, hobbled in the yard, surrounded by grass plucked that morning.

Carolyn found such dilemmas boring. Couldn't he accept things as they were, and not think so much? The blazing light had brought on one of her headaches, not a little aggravated by the sight of him brooding. She sat in the car while he took more pictures. Even as he did, his pleasure in it was diminished by the knowledge that Carolyn would argue with him about the slides. In her opinion he forgot where he had been; she did not. "To hear Ralph," she would say, "you would think I hadn't been on the trip!" Actually, it was true in a way she would never admit. Those walks Ralph took while Carolyn napped were often the source of his finest shots. "I'm sure he bought that one somewhere," she would say. "I never saw such a place."

These depressing reflections, like Carolyn's headaches, often occurred on those days that "were out of this world," and indicated that they both suffered from too much light. In such euphoric situations they helped Ralph keep his feet on the ground. When he came back to the car, it was surrounded by sheep and Carolyn had run her window up for protection. He could see Carolyn speaking to him, but the bleating of the lambs drowned out what she said. Ralph was disturbed, as he was so often, by the meaning of a scene that seemed to escape him, just as her open mouth spoke words to him that he

130

failed to hear. In this instance she would accuse him of thinking more of his silly pictures than of her safety, using as his excuse this talk about how safe it was in Spain. Carolyn didn't mean these things, she simply found it a relief to talk.

As they climbed toward Ronda, Ralph tried to recall some of the high points of Hemingway's description, but it seemed to be a large impression made up of very few details. That was the art of it. If the gorge he spoke about was a mile deep, it meant the city itself would be a mile high. There was a possibility that Carolyn, who was sensitive to heights, might feel a bit queasy and not want to eat. The actual approach was not at all exciting, but it freshly prepared them for the view from the window of their hotel. Absolutely dazzling: Carolyn stepped back from it with a gasp. Ralph took a roll of shots right there in the room so she would be able to enjoy the view later, safe at home. The altitude left Carolyn bushed, however, and she settled for a nap while Ralph peered around. Three busloads of German tourists—in buses so huge Ralph marveled how they had ever got up there— crowded the aisles of the small gift shop and gathered in clusters in the patio garden. Many of them, like Carolyn and Ralph, had come to Ronda with a purpose, which was why one saw them huddled in silence before the life-size statue of Rilke. That in itself surprised Ralph. What had ever brought Rilke to a place like this? He was one of the people Carolyn read and liked so much better than Mr. Hemingway. Rilke would never think of bolting with anybody to such a public spectacle. Ralph's pleasure at the thought of informing Carolyn that her sensitive poet had his statue in the garden was diminished by the fact that he had come here thirteen years before Ralph had been born, and ahead of Hemingway. Ronda was an old tourist mecca, really, and the English and the Germans had been coming here for ages. How had Hemingway convinced him he had more or less discovered it?

When the Germans had departed Ralph had the garden and the view to himself. More than a mile below, lamplight glowed in the windows of the farmhouses. It was like another country, cut off and remote from the one on the rim. Down there it had been dark for an hour or more; here where Ralph stood the sun flamed on the windows. Ralph took a picture of the one behind which Carolyn slept. It would be hard for her to refute something like that. Several wide brick paths crisscrossed the garden, and one went along the rim, with bays for viewing. In every direction the prospect seemed staggering. In their first years of marriage Ralph had schemed to get Carolyn, somehow, to Arizona, and by stealth, driving at night, up to Bright Angel Lodge on the rim of the Canyon. In the morning she would wake up to face that awesome sight. Her own feeling was that she had come too late for great spectacles. Fellini movies and travel pictures had spoiled it for her. Ralph couldn't seem to understand that actually *being* there, under these circumstances, merely led to a letdown. She would just as soon miss whatever it was as feel something like that.

The path Ralph followed ended so abruptly that he found himself facing a high cable fence, while still preoccupied with his reflections. The two wings of the gate were locked with a chain, but Ralph could see that the path still continued. Weeds grew over it now, and the wall along the rim had breaks here and there that made it dangerous, but in Hemingway's time—not to mention Rilke's—people who came to Ronda did not stop at this fence. They had not come all this way to be fenced in. The tourist walked in those days, he was known as a traveler, and he did not climb from a bus to sit in a bar, or spend a frenzied half-hour in the gift shop. He got out

132

and looked around. He wanted his money's worth. Ralph was not so crass, but he had not come to Ronda to peer through a fence. He had not come with that in mind, but as so often happened that was what he was doing, his fingers hooked in the wires, his eyes at one of the holes. Otherwise he would never have noticed the figure seated on the wall some fifty yards ahead. It was warm there. The sun, in fact, had moved from his lap to his chest and shoulders. He seemed to sit for the portrait that Ralph would like to take. He wore the wide wale corduroy, with the comfortably loose jacket, the pockets large, the back belted, that Ralph had seen on men he judged to be groundskeepers, guides, watchmen, or whatever. He gave Ralph a nod and a quick smile—free of all "at your service" intimations. Like Ralph, he was a man enjoying the scene. Ralph also thought him so rustically handsome he would like to have a shot of him for Carolyn. Among other things, it would give the scene scale. On second thought it crossed his mind that just such a picture might be available in the hotel lobby. The fellow held a stick, or a cane, in such a manner one knew it was part of his habit, tapping it idly on the hobnailed sole of his boot.

When Ralph remained at the fence, as if expecting to enter, the man rose and came toward him, flicking the weeds with his stick. He greeted Ralph in Spanish and, as if he had been asked, unlocked the chain that closed the gate. He then gestured—in the manner of a man who works with children, or clusters of tourists—for Ralph to come along with him. Concealed beneath the overgrowth was a hard stone path that he followed out of long habit, his eyes up ahead. Ralph trailed along behind him, rising slowly to an elevation once cleared but now strewn with boulders from collapsed walls. The view from here—at this hour of the day—looked south along the canyon like the sea's bottom, the upper slopes flaming with a light like the glow from a furnace door. Where had Ralph seen it before? In the inferno paintings of Breughel and Bosch. At once, that is, indescribable and terrifying. Ralph had no word for it, and apparently none was expected. His companion stood, dyed in the same flaming color, facing what appeared to be left the instant following the act of creation, while the earth still cooled. Swallows nested in the cliffs, and their cries could be heard, changing in pitch as they shifted direction. Their flight on the sky was like fine scratches on film. After a moment of silence the man turned his head and appeared to be surprised that Ralph merely stood there. His eye moved from his face to the camera on his chest.

"No pictures?"

Smilingly, Ralph shrugged. Wasn't it almost impertinent to think that anything but the eye might catch it? The canyon had darkened even as they stood there, as if filling with an inky fluid, rising on the slopes. At the bottom a sinuous road was the exact metallic color of the sky, like the belly of a snake. No, Ralph was not so foolish to believe he could catch it on film. His companion, however, was puzzled.

"No feeelm?" he asked.

Oh, yes, Ralph had film. He nodded to indicate the camera was loaded; he was just not taking any pictures. This aroused the man's interest. He tilted his head in the manner of the querulous, credulous tourist, looking sharply at Ralph. Was he something new? If he had not come to Ronda for pictures, what then? Ralph sensed his question clearly enough, but he could do no more than stand there. His position was not easily explained. He attempted, with some strain, to indicate that he "was taking it all in with his eyes" rather than his lens. Did it help? The man continued to eye him—a good honest man, Ralph thought, but perhaps a little simple in his thinking. People came here to take pictures. Why didn't Ralph do what was expected of him?

What Ralph *did* do—to distract his gaze, to do something if not take pictures—was remove from his pocket the bar of chocolate he had brought all the way from Madrid. Swiss bitter chocolate, the best; something this sensible fellow would have a taste for. The piece Ralph offered he accepted, with *muchas gracias*. Chewing up the piece, he was led to comment that he knew Swiss chocolate, and judged it superior. The Swiss made chocolate and watches. He extended toward Ralph a thick, hairy wrist, ornamented with a watch of Swiss manufacture. The one Ralph then exposed to him received his respectful, somewhat awed, admiration. Such an object with dials and levers he had had heard about, but not seen. It is a commonplace of travel experience that absolute strangers have these congenial moments—not in spite of, but rather because of, their brevity. With the second piece of chocolate his friend suggested—this was the feeling of the moment—that they take seats on the boulders and enjoy the last of the sunset. Knees high, the leveling sun in their eyes, they finished off the chocolate. Ralph observed how, as his companion peeled off the foil, he put the wad of wrapping in his pocket. Overhead were the swallows. Nearer at hand Ralph was conscious of bats. Fortunately, Carolyn was not present to destroy this moment with hysterical shrieking, believing, as she did, that bats were no more than horrible flying mice.

Four or five minutes? Ten at the most? Now and then they idly glanced at the display before them, as gods might be amused by the northern lights. On the cliffs the remarkable tints seemed to bleed and dry like watercolors. His friend was the first to rise—not without a groan —and extend toward Ralph a helping hand. Why should something so common be so memorable? In his brusque matter-of-factness Ralph sensed that he too felt it. He was not so simple he did not know that this moment was something special. They walked back toward the hotel, the man ahead, Ralph trailing, turning once for a last glance at what vanished as they were looking. In that instant, it seemed, the air turned cold. They continued to the gate, where Ralph, in an involuntary gesture, turned and placed his left hand on the man's shoulder, and offered him his right. His companion lowered his eyes as if to locate Ralph's hand in the darkness. Yes, he actually looked. It seemed so droll a thing to do—something you might expect from a natural comic—that Ralph actually smiled. He also reached for the hand that was partially offered, gripped it firmly, then said *Vaya con dios*—only one of many things he would soon enough regret. The man muttered something, but Ralph was so moved by his own feelings, his own generous impulses, he heard nothing but the wind of his own emotion.

Fortunately, the gate had been opened, and he was able to turn and make his escape. *Make his escape?* Was that the first suspicion that he had misread the situation? He did not look back. The fresh smarting of his face, a warmness all over his body, was not the result of his downhill walking. No, he was blushing. He was overheated with embarrassment. So clear to him now he could only go along with his head down, thankful for the darkness, was that this man had looked to his hand for something Ralph had not offered. A payment for services rendered.

Least of all the things in this world he had expected, or wanted, was a handshake. A *handshake!* He must be standing there, shaking with laughter. This Americano who offered him a handshake? Was it believable? He would now go home with empty pockets but a story, a tale, that would last forever, be repeated by his children, conceivably become a legend of sorts at Ronda. The big Americano tourist who had gripped his hand,

and urged him to go with God.

From a niche behind the statue of Rilke, Ralph paused long enough for a quick glance rearward. Had he gone? No, he was still there, but the rising tide of darkness had submerged him. He was all of one color, at this distance, his face the weathered tan of his corduroy, but Ralph had the distinct impression that his teeth were exposed in a smile. That could have been wrong. Maybe he merely stood there stupefied. Ralph might have walked, unseen, into the lobby, where the lights were now on, a fire was burning, and the woman who stood before it, warming her backside, wore a mini-skirt. Was it something he could speak about to Carolyn? How would it be phrased? Would she understand his failure to grasp he was in another country? And if not where he was, *how things were?* This man had done him a service—could it have been more obvious? He had opened a gate and given him a short tour—and on the return Ralph had offered him his hand. Would it be sensible, would it be believable, that Ralph considered him an equal, such a fleeting but true friend, really, that to have offered him money would have falsified their brief meeting, and reduced something gold to something brass? Carolyn would only make one of those gargle sounds in her throat. The other thing was —a sudden chill brought it home—that what he had been thinking of all the time was the high value of his own sensations, and in this intoxication he felt these sensations would be shared with his companion. As Ralph valued him, surely he would be moved to value Ralph, a fumbling but generous tourist who in a kind of Eucharist offered him chocolate. In this brief wordless drama two illusions had suffered, but was there any doubt whose had been the greater? Both stories were good, but Ralph's would be one he kept to himself.

1972

137

Fiona

In England, where Fiona felt free, she would tie the
sleeves of a sweater about her waist, fill the pockets of
her tunic with Fig Newtons, then clop for hours through
a landscape green as the sea and almost as wet. She loved
the pelt of rain on her hair, the splatter of it on her face.
This rain did not pour. It hung like a vapor that settled
on her skin and smoked in her lungs. Trotting and walking, the drizzle steaming her face, her legs sliced with the
drag and tangle of the grass, those who heard her coming
or going said that she sounded like a winded horse. How
that made her laugh! From these wet runs she would
return to her room soaked to the skin, too exhausted to

sleep, like one of the small watery cubs of Beowulf's dam, escaped from the deep. That's her own description. The one subject she never tires of is herself.

Time would prove that nothing else would arouse in Fiona such a full awareness of her flesh as a piece of nature. Sex didn't. In her opinion, strange as it seems, there was too much in sex that was *im*material. All of the sentiment, for one thing. Then all of the mess. Fiona didn't blather it to the world, but she took for *granted* the primacy of the spirit. That seemed obvious. The difficult and the beautiful thing was to make the spirit flesh. That common practice would see it just the other way around was a flaw in man, not in nature, and the major flaw in man—she would add with a guffaw—was the one she had married. A joke? That was how people took it. Including Charles, the one she had married. Fiona's strident, horsy laugh is surprising in a woman of her cultivation. Seated, she rocks back and forth, slapping her knees. One sees the teeth she has missing and the dark cave at the back of her mouth. So the gods must laugh at men, and in the same spirit Fiona laughs at the gods. Who else can be held responsible? On their last trip to the coast (they took a Pullman) the porter had assumed that the man along with her, in his cap and sports jacket, *had* to be her son. What could she do but laugh? She had learned to live with it, but what she found a strain was how his weakness seemed to give him strength. Life clung to him. He lacked even the strength to fight it off. Every day of her life it was forced upon Fiona that this hapless man she had married would survive her. The older he became the younger he looked. If he wore his tennis sneakers and went out without his hat, students at the college took him for an instructor. Some of the girls swooned to learn that he read Greek. With a few

139

exceptions, only Fiona could appreciate the humor of her situation, the love of folly being the last, great love of her life.

Somehow the first question Fiona is asked is where in the world, and how, she met Charles. Why will take time. It is not felt necessary to ask where in the world Charles met Fiona. Perhaps he didn't. It is obvious that Fiona met him. This question is a natural at the yearly fall parties introducing new members of the department. Fiona, who is pouring tea, will be seated. Charles stands —somehow he is always standing—an erect, handsome man, scholarly, cultivated, his face little changed from the day Fiona met him thirty years ago. That can't be, of course, but it is. Charles wears caps, does not wear glasses unless he sits reading, has the attractive smattering of gray hair of a young college man. No wrinkles. A seam where his head joins his neck. He stands, thighs pressed together, holding in one cupped palm an elbow, in the other a silver-rimmed glass with three ice cubes and his first stint of daily bourbon. If any, the water comes from the ice. If witty and effusive, Charles is tight, and capable of a very misleading performance. His manner, and the Oxford accent that time has not eroded, lead people to correctly think that Fiona met him in England. It is never easy for them to accept that Charles was born in Indiana, just thirty miles north of Pickett, where he attended a school so backward he was able to major in Greek. This had more than a little to do with his being chosen as a Rhodes scholar; being chosen by Fiona shortly followed. They were married in France.

Charles will go on to tell you—if Fiona hasn't—that in his second year at Oxford, on a walking tour with a companion, he stopped to watch two teams of girls club each other nearly senseless. The game was lacrosse. The most proficient clubber of the lot was Fiona. But at that very moment she was getting hers with a sharp crack on the elbow. For the cello (she planned a career in music) she exchanged Charles, as simple as that. Broad in the shoulders and hips, long-limbed and large-boned, a mane of chestnut hair in two pigtails, Fiona Copley personified the spirit of Sparta that seemed to be absent from the study of the classics. There is a snapshot of Charles, taken on that excursion, standing just to one side of the Amazon, Fiona, that sums up in a glance the new world that is born, and the world that is gone. His arms are folded on his chest. His finger marks the place in a book of Housman's poems. If Housman's brook proved too broad for leaping, it was not entirely Charles's decision. At the sound of the word "leap," he had leaped. Was it at that moment he first experienced, or suffered, Fiona's laugh? Uninhibited, laced with fragments of what she happened to be chewing, it is not now, nor was it then, unusual for Fiona to almost choke to death. The only cure is several thumps, with the flat of the hand, on her broad back. Both friends and colleagues not so friendly have had occasion to thump Fiona. She takes it in good spirits. It often starts her laughing again. Flushed with coughing, her face red and perspiring, she will glance up at Charles, who stands tunelessly whistling, or toying with one of the cubes in his drink.

"I believe he'd let me choke rather than thump me!" she will cry, and this often leads to another fit of coughing. It is the truth that makes Fiona laugh, never mind what it is.

Neither a pretty girl nor a womanly woman—even her abundant hair is like a barrister's wig—Fiona resembles a well-endowed but obvious female impersonator. Her feet are large, her strides are that of Piers Plowman in foot-molded shoes. If she came at the wrong time, and in the wrong country, nevertheless she came to the right school. Her music festivals attract the gifted, fussy people who consider Aspen too high, Lucerne too far, and the Berkshires too close. They have precisely the taste and quaint cultivated madness to enjoy Charles's slides of the Crusader castles, a subject on which they will admit him to be the authority. For thirty-one years he has been at work on the text. It can be idly examined in the whisky cartons that line one wall of his study: they stack well, and he can always assume they contain something else. Scholarly books in Greek and Latin, bound in vellum, stuffed like wallets with cards and notations, occupy the table, the chairs, and the bed where Charles does his sleeping and reading. Every year, for twelve years, a scholarly press advertised the book and took orders for it, then announced a brief delay in its publication. Some scholars hold the opinion the work is published, but hard to find. The work keeps him happy. More important, it keeps him out of the way. Fiona has a lively interest in people, and will sometimes say that she *collects* men. Their wives are always told there is no reason to worry, and they don't.

Before settling down Fiona and Charles had lived everywhere one could do it cheaply. Majorca first, of course, and then the Costa Brava. After Ibiza to Rhodes, where Charles continued his exhaustive researches into Crusader castles, and from there to Corfu, to Mykonos, to Dubrovnik, then to Minorca and the Canaries, a winter in Madeira, and several summers island-hopping, in and out of known and unknown villas on which Fiona left the impression of royalty in exile. This characteristic had the effect of enlarging her past and diminishing her future. It was seldom asked where she was off to—merely where she had been. The whack on the elbow had scotched a career, but it could hardly be said it ruined her talent. On an income of less than three thousand a year, with introductions to people who sat waiting for them, they managed to be warm when it was freezing and reasonably cool when it was stifling, living with people but not strictly off them, and always remarkably independent. In those years the London office of the Oxford Press—with other offices in Bombay, Calcutta, and elsewhere—received further material on a volume that would be definitive if it was ever completed.

No matter what island, Charles was up early, Fiona slept late. Her quality showed to its greatest advantage in her mastery of leisure. She detested committees, cultivated no hobbies, and showed no interest in world- or self-improvement. Charles did his writing in the morning, and after lunch they would take a long walk together: their hosts impatiently waited for the clop of their hobbled boots on the porch. Both wore hiking shoes, carried binoculars, canes, biscuits, and bars of bitter Swiss chocolate. Chocolate kept Fiona going as she waited for Charles to determine where.

On their honeymoon—a walking tour of the Alps—Fiona had insisted on visiting the tiny village of Coppet, noted as the burial place of Madame de Staël. That seemed understandable. Fiona had much in common with a woman of her temperament and talents. Charles knew the usual things about Madame de Staël but he had not heard the story about her mother, Madame Necker. She did not have her daughter's assortment of talents, nor did she dream, like her daughter, of an enduring fame. Yet she had her dream. In some respects a very ambitious one. Madame Necker did not want to *live* forever, but she did want to survive. Not in the hearts and minds of men, like her child, but in the sweet, solid flesh on her own bones. Death she did not fear. Physical disintegration she did. To die she was willing—to turn to food for worms she was not. Over the years she had observed, like many people, that actual bodies were preserved in large stoppered bottles, where they floated in the clear, immortal broth of alcohol. If this could be done for God's smaller creatures, why not for a large one like Madame Necker? All one needed was a bottle, or a cask, big enough. So she had one made, a huge glass-lined cask large enough for both Madame Necker and her husband. It was filled with alcohol. Soon enough, it floated the remains of the Neckers, and by draining off an appropriate quantity of the liquid, room was made, in time, for Madame de Staël. It was this excess liquid—according to tradition, and as recounted to Charles by Fiona— that was used to fortify the local vintage, and make it much in demand.

On such a story such a twist was to be expected, but who could guess that Fiona would never tire of it? Nor did her listeners, the way she could tell it. It often left her gasping and choking, tears of laughter in her eyes. Only Charles, who lacked Fiona's strong stomach, seemed to be a little sensitive about it. His comment was that the story betrayed her original but somewhat perverse ancestor worship. She had replied that it was no such thing: it was pure self-love. Nor was she the first to cherish the fat on her own bones. Self-love seemed to Fiona—as she never tired of saying—much less perverse than other forms of love with which she was familiar, a comment that diverted the discussion to other things.

I need to emphasize that Fiona's self-love has little to do with matters of the spirit. She is the first to point out that the spirit is free to shift for itself—it's her too solid flesh that gives her the willies. Into dust or worse? She won't accept it. The important point is, she no longer has to. All of that is part of the past—one large past—that she has put behind her. The discovery and perfection of the modern freezing unit—at about the time she was at school in England—made it possible for Fiona to be practical as well as ambitious. Survival in the flesh was no problem. The problems now were in the field of thawing out.

This obsession—or passion, if you prefer it—has its origin in her childhood. One winter Fiona, with her brother Ronald, skated on a millpond near the house. It's still there: one of many nuisances she refuses to give up. The first freeze of winter had left the pond ice clear as glass. Fiona didn't skate too well, as a child, and spent most of the time on her hands and knees, peering into the ice. On that day she saw, just a few inches beneath her, the wide staring eyes of a life-size doll, frozen in the ice. The lips were parted. She felt it might speak back if she spoke to it. She called to her brother and they stood there considering how to get the doll out of the ice. Ronald ran to the house, and returned with a sled and a saw that his father used to remove blocks of ice in the spring. After a great deal of effort they lugged the block home on Ronald's sled. As the ice quickly thawed in a tub of warm water the doll's lovely hair spread out on the surface. A moment later Fiona was able to free one of the chubby pink hands. Ronald says that she shrieked like a wild bird at the touch. This doll's hand was that of a recently drowned child. It had been so perfectly preserved in the ice that Fiona believed it must still be alive. It took time to convince her. She was convinced that it merely slept, and would speak to her when it thawed. The thaw, unfortunately, soon occurred, and she watched the flawlessly beautiful eyes dissolve like ice cubes and run down the cheeks like tears.

Such an experience is not easily forgotten. For a child like Fiona it was crucial. It provided her, as she admits herself, with the key to her own nature. Survival was what she wanted: survival in the flesh. This bizarre expe-

145

rience had revealed to her how it might be done.

For Charles, the crucial revelation was his brief acquaintance with Madame Necker, floating in the huge cask in Coppet. There he saw for himself how well alcohol preserved the flesh. He accepted the proof, but preferred to take it internally. When the time came to die he would be so well pickled he would require only framing.

As it applied to Charles, Fiona came to be fond of the word *pickled*. Charles is pickled, she would say, to explain his occasional absence, or the way he might stand, the glass cupped in his palm, blowing softly on the ice cubes as if to thaw them, a dimpled, archaic smile on his moist lips.

For all her love of alcohol, Fiona does not drink. Neither does she smoke, but for years her health has not been good. Her hair is white, several joints are stiffening, and there will soon be little solid flesh to preserve on the bones.

For all that he drinks, Charles's health appears to be good. He is one of those men who seem to be preserved in the very liquid that destroys so many others. His teeth are white. He has a thick pelt of hair. True enough, he does have the shakes, which is why he holds the glass in such a curious manner, the cubes tinkling as he stands like a good whisky ad with his back to the fire. It is one thing to be pickled, briefly, while alive: quite another to be pickled, and bottled, forever. It's the *forever* that bugs him, and helps explain his apparent good health.

To have nothing to fear but fear itself, Charles will tell you, is more than sufficient. For one thing, pure fear is inexhaustible. For another, the age has caught up with Charles, after so long being safely behind him. Once only alcohol would preserve what seemed to matter. Now there is dry ice. It took a few thousand years and great quantities of ice to preserve the woolly mammoth in the wastes of Siberia, but this could currently be done at small expense in a frozen-food locker. It is Fiona's idea that a huge floating freezer would have served much better than Noah's ark. In the freezer, two of every kind of creature would still be as fresh as the day they were frozen, with more than a fifty-fifty chance of being thawed and put back into circulation. In the basement of her home Fiona has her own freezer, one six feet six inches long and forty inches wide. That is large enough for her: to prove it she will stretch out in it for you, the metallic walls of the box magnifying her remarkably resonant laughter. Does she plan on just lying there forever? Why not? Just in case the power might go off during an electric storm, or an air raid, she has installed a power plant that operates on its own gasoline motor. Charles—who still looks as young as ever—will be around to supervise and keep things going. If by chance he isn't, the box is also large enough for him. One of her expanding programs, now gathering members, is concerned with continued Freezer Survival, and will supply the organization and funds necessary to keep the current flowing. Everybody knows the idea of his dying first is what keeps Charles looking so young. Fiona makes him nervous, but he is the one with the black head of hair, she with the white one. Charles has the air of breeding that makes it unnecessary for him to talk very much. He stands a good deal, his back to the fireplace, or moves about whatever room he is in looking for new or old timepieces. He has a thing about clocks. Battery-driven ones interest him less than those activated by atmospheric pressure, or run by weights. The ticking that many find so aggravating appeals to Charles. He likes the modern clocks with the visible movements, or the older type with the pendulum rocking, perhaps a smaller dial on the face notching off the seconds. Time. What the devil is it?—Charles will ask. Since everybody knows he is a student of the subject the question is rhetorical, to say the least. It is a fiction, surely, having no meaning beyond the measurement of the past. Otherwise it is merely a form of the future tense. That simple, ticking hand of the clock indicates something that defies comprehension. Something that never was, for a moment is, and is as suddenly gone. In Fiona, for example, time ticks away in a visible, even audible, measure. In Charles, oddly enough, it appears to have stopped. An illusion, of course, as the beat of his heart can be seen in the tremor of his hand, or, when he is seated, in the wagging toe of his boot. If time is not the movement of one thing or another, has it stopped? If, indeed, a low point of freezing brings all movement to a standstill, can it be said, or proven, that time exists? Queries like that get from Fiona one of her memorable, infectious guffaws. The erosion of time can be seen at both the back and front of her mouth. Doesn't she care? She behaves like a player with the trump card. For all of her remarkable talents she sometimes seems a little simple-minded. Or on the mad side —whichever side that is. The latitude in these matters merely points up what we know to be the gist of the problem. On a subject of interest, of life and death, does anybody really know anything of importance? Just who is dying, for example, is as hard to determine as who is living. It is in the courts. We no longer know for sure when a person is dead.

Three days ago, now, Charles was found lying face up in the freezer as if he had dropped there. He was frozen stiff. That is all that can be said for certain: he is frozen stiff. Fiona will not allow the authorities to thaw him out. The one thing that is known for certain in these matters is that you can't refreeze what has once been thawed, and this is neither the time nor the place to bring Charles back for interrogation. If a better world was what he had in mind, this is not it.

Something will have to be done, sooner or later, but Fiona has threatened to sue for murder any person or persons who thaw Charles out. Until he is thawed, who can say what remains to be said? There is another school of thought on the matter, which suggests a period of watchful waiting. Why not? There is little or nothing that can happen to Charles. Ten years from now he will still be as he is. The authorities have adopted the position of watch and wait. Some believe it safe to assume, from her present appearance, that Fiona will not long survive him, and at the time of her death such legal steps as are found necessary might be taken. She is the one who laughs when she considers what they might be. I could be wrong, of course, but my impression is that Fiona is looking better than ever, now that Charles—that is, his future—has been taken care of. She looks younger. With a little persuasion she will join you for a drink.

1970

The Safe Place

In his fifty-third year a chemical blast burned the beard from the Colonel's face, and gave to his eyes their characteristic powdery blue. Sometime later his bushy eyebrows came in white. Silvery streaks of the same color appeared in his hair. To his habitually bored expression these touches gave a certain distinction, a man-of-the-world air, which his barber turned to the advantage of his face. The thinning hair was parted, the lock of silver was deftly curled. The Colonel had an absent-minded way of stroking it back. As he was self-conscious, rather than vain, there was something attractive about this gesture, and a great pity that women didn't seem to interest him. He had married one to reassure himself on that point.

When not away at war the Colonel lived with his wife in an apartment on the Heights, in Brooklyn. She lived at the front with her canary, Jenny Lind, and he lived at the back with his two cats. His wife did not care for cats, particularly, but she had learned to accept the situation, just as the cats had learned, when the Colonel was absent, to shift for themselves. The cleaning women, as a rule, were tipped liberally to be attentive to them. The Colonel supplied the cats with an artificial tree, which they could climb, claw, or puzzle over, and a weekly supply of fresh catnip mice. The mice were given to the cats every Thursday, as on Friday the cleaning woman, with a broom and the vacuum, would try to get the shredded catnip out of the rug. They would then settle back and wait patiently for Thursday again.

The blast improved the Colonel's looks, but it had not been so good for his eyes. They watered a good deal, the pupils were apt to dilate in a strange manner, and he became extremely sensitive to light. In the sun he didn't see any too well. To protect his eyes from the light he wore a large pair of military glasses, with dark lenses, and something like blinders at the sides. He was wearing these glasses when he stepped from the curbing, in uptown Manhattan, and was hit by a pie truck headed south. He was put in the back, with the pies, and carted to a hospital.

He hovered between life and death for several weeks. Nor was there any explanation as to why he pulled through. He had nothing to live for, and his health was not good. In the metal locker at the foot of the bed was the uniform in which he had been delivered, broken up, as the doctor remarked, like a sack of crushed ice. The uniform, however, had come through rather well. There were a few stains, but no bad tears or rips. It had been carefully cleaned, and now hung in the locker waiting for him.

The Colonel, however, showed very little interest in getting up. He seemed to like it, as his wife remarked, well enough in bed. When he coughed, a blue vein would crawl from his hair and divide his forehead, and the salty tears brimming in his weak eyes would stream down his face. He had aged, he was not really alive, but he refused to die. After several weeks he was therefore removed from the ward of hopeless cases, and put among those who were said to have a fifty-fifty chance. Visitors came to this room, and there were radios. From his bed there was a fine view of the city including the East River, the Brooklyn Bridge, part of lower Manhattan, and the harbor from which the Colonel had never sailed. With his military glasses he could see the apartment where his wife and cats lived. On the roofs of the tenements that sprawled below there daily appeared, like a plague of Martian insects, the television aerials that brought to the poor the empty lives of the rich. The Colonel ordered a set, but was told that his failing eyes were too weak.

On the table at his side were a glass of water, boxes of vitamin capsules and pills, an expensive silver lighter, and a blurred photograph of his cats. A bedpan and a carton of cigarettes were on the shelf beneath. The Colonel had a taste for expensive cigarettes, in tins of fifty, or small cedar boxes, but his pleasure seemed to be in the lighter, which required no flint. The small gas cartridge would light, it was said, many thousand cigarettes. As it made no sound, the Colonel played with it at night. During the day he lit many cigarettes and let them smoke in the room, like incense, but during the night he experimented with the small wiry hairs on his chest.

152

Several twisted together, and ignited, would give off a crackling sound. It pleased him to singe the blonde hairs on his fingers, hold them to his nose. When not playing with the lighter the Colonel slept, or sat for hours with an air of brooding, or used his army glasses to examine the teeming life in the streets. What he saw, however, was no surprise to him. To an old army man it was just another bloody battlefield.

In his fifty-third year, having time on his hands, the Colonel was able to see through the glasses what he had known, so to speak, all his life. Life, to put it simply, was a battleground. Every living thing, great or small, spilled its blood on it. Every day he read the uproar made in the press about the horrors of war, the fear of the draft, and what it would do to the lives of the fresh eighteen-year-olds. Every moment he could see a life more horrible in the streets. Dangers more unjust, risks more uncalculated, and barracks that were more intolerable. Children fell from windows, were struck by cars in the street, were waylaid and corrupted by evil old men, or through some private evil crawled off to corrupt themselves. Loose boards rose up and struck idle women, knives cut their fingers, fire burned their clothes, or in some useless quarrel they suffered heart attacks. The ambulance appeared after every holiday. The sirens moaned through the streets, like specters, every night. Doors closed on small fingers, windows fell, small dogs bit bigger dogs, or friends and neighbors, and in the full light of day a man would tumble, head first, down the steps to the street. If this man was a neighbor they might pick him up, but if a stranger they would pass him by, walking in an arc around him the way children swing wide of a haunted house. Or they would stand in a circle, blocking the walk, until the man who was paid to touch a dead man felt the wrist for the pulse, or held the pocket mirror to the face. As if the dead man, poor devil, wanted a final look at himself.

All of this struck the Colonel, an old soldier, as a new kind of battleground. "That's life for you," the doctor would say, when the Colonel would trouble to point out that the only safe place for a man, or a soldier, was in bed. Trapped there, so to speak, and unable to get up and put on his pants. For it was with his pants that a man put on the world. He became a part of it, he accepted the risks and the foolishness. The Colonel could see this very clearly in the casualties brought to the ward, the men who had fallen on this nameless battlefield. They lay staring at the same world that seemed to terrify the Colonel, but not one of these men was at all disturbed by it. Everything they saw seemed to appeal to them. Every woman reminded them of their wives, and every child of their own children, and the happy times, the wonderful life they seemed to think they had lived. When another victim appeared in the ward they would cry out to ask him "How are things going?" although it was clear things were still going murderously. That it was worth a man's life to put on his pants and appear in the streets. But not one of these men, broken and battered as they were, by the world they had left, had any other thought but a craving to get back to it. To be broken, battered, and bruised all over again. The Colonel found it hard to believe his eyes—both inside and outside the window— as the world of men seemed to be incomprehensible. It affected, as he knew it would, his feeble will to live. He did not die, but neither did he live, as if the world both inside and outside the window was a kind of purgatory, a foretaste of hell but with no possibility of heaven. Once a week his wife, a small attractive woman who referred to him as Mr. Army, brought him cookies made with blackstrap molasses, pure brewer's yeast, and wheat-germ flour. The recipe was her own, but they were made by the cleaning woman. As Mrs. Porter was several years older than the Colonel, and looked from eight to ten years younger, there was no need to argue the importance of blackstrap and brewer's yeast. The Colonel would ask how the cats were doing, read the mail she had brought him, and when she had left he would distribute the cookies in the ward. A young man named Hyman Kopfman was fond of them.

Hyman Kopfman was a small, rabbit-faced little man who belonged in the hopeless ward, but it had been overcrowded and he couldn't afford a room of his own. When he appeared in the ward he had one leg and two arms, but before the first month had ended they had balanced him up, as he put it himself. He stored the cookies away in the sleeve of the arm that he wore pinned up. Something in Hyman Kopfman's blood couldn't live with the rest of Hyman Kopfman, and he referred to this thing as America. Raising the stump of his leg he would say, "Now you're seeing America first!" Then he would laugh. He seemed to get a great kick out of it. Largely because of Hyman Kopfman, there were men in the ward, some of them pretty battered, who looked on the world outside as a happy place. Only the Colonel seemed to see the connection. He didn't know what Hyman Kopfman had in his blood, or where it would show up next, but he knew that he had picked it up, like they all did, there in the streets. What Hyman Kopfman knew was that the world was killing him.

Hyman Kopfman was in pain a good deal of the time and sat leaning forward, his small head in his hand, like a man who was contemplating a crystal globe. During the night he often rocked back and forth, creaking the springs. While the Colonel sat playing with his lighter, Hyman Kopfman would talk, as if to himself, but he seemed to be aware that the Colonel was listening. Hyman Kopfman's way of passing the time was not to look at the world through a pair of field glasses, but to turn his gaze, so to speak, upon himself. Then to describe in considerable detail what he saw. As the Colonel was a reserved, reticent man who considered his life and experience private, Hyman Kopfman was something of a novelty. He spoke of himself as if he were somebody else. There were even times when the Colonel thought he was. At the start Hyman Kopfman gave the impression that he would describe everything that had happened; which he did, perhaps, but all that had happened had not added up to much. He was apt to repeat certain things time and time again. There were nights when the Colonel had the impression that he went over the same material the way a wine press went over the pulp of grapes. But there was always something that refused to squeeze out. That, anyhow, was the Colonel's impression, since it was otherwise hard to explain why he went over the same material time and again; here and there adding a touch, or taking one away.

Hyman Kopfman had been born in Vienna—that was what he said. That should have been of some interest in itself, and as the Colonel had never been to Vienna, he always listened in the hope that he might learn something. But Hyman Kopfman merely talked about himself. He might as well have been born in the Bronx, or anywhere else. He had been a frail boy with girlish wrists and pale blue hands, as he said himself, but with something hard to explain that made him likable. His father had it, but only his mother knew what it was. Hopelessness. It was this, he said, that made him lovable.

The Colonel got awfully tired of this part of the story since Hyman Kopfman was hopeless enough. Too hopeless, in fact. There was nothing about him that was lova-

156

ble. It was one of the curious conceits he had. His skin was a pale doughy color, and his general health was so poor that when he smiled his waxy gums began to bleed. Thin streaks of red, like veins in marble, showed on his chalky teeth. His eyes were very large, nearly goatlike, with curiously transparent lids, as if the skin had been stretched very thin to cover them. There were times when the eyes, with their large wet whites and peculiarly dilated pupils, gazed upon the Colonel with a somewhat luminous quality. It was disturbing, and had to do, very likely, with his poor health. It was because of his eyes, the Colonel decided, that Hyman Kopfman had picked up the notion that there was something appealing about his hopelessness. Some woman, perhaps his mother, had told him that.

At a very early age Hyman Kopfman had been brought to America. With him came his three brothers, his mother, Frau Tabori-Kopfman, and the room full of furniture and clothes that his father had left to them. They went to live in Chicago, where his Uncle Tabori, his mother's brother, had rented an apartment. This apartment was four flights up from the street with a room at the back for Uncle Tabori, a room at the front, called a parlor, and a room in which they lived. In the parlor there were large bay windows but the curtains were kept closed as the light and the circulating air would fade the furniture. It would belong to Paul, the elder brother, when he married someone. In the room were chests full of clothes that his mother had stopped wearing, and his father, a gentleman, had never worn out. They were still as good as new. So it was up to the children to wear them out. It so happened that Mandel Kopfman, the father, had been comparatively small in stature, and his fine clothes would fit Hyman Kopfman, but nobody else. So it was that Hyman Kopfman was accustomed to wear, as he walked between the bedroom and the bathroom, pants of very good cloth, and on his small feet the best grade of spats. French braces held up his pants, and there was also a silver-headed cane, with a sword in the shaft, that he sometimes carried as he swaggered down the hall. He didn't trouble, of course, to go down the four flights to the street. Different clothes were being worn down there, small tough boys cursed and shouted, and once down, Hyman Kopfman would have to walk back up. He simply couldn't. He never had the strength.

His older brother, Otto, went down all the time as he worked down there, in a grocery, and returned to tell them what it was all about. He also went to movies, and told them about that. At that time his brother Paul had been too young to go down to the street and work there, so he made the beds and helped his mother around the house. He cooked, he learned to sew, and as he couldn't wear the clothes of Mandel Kopfman, he wore some of the skirts and blouses of his mother, as they fit him all right. It didn't matter, as he never left the rooms. No one but Uncle Tabori ever sat down and talked with them. He worked in the railroad yards that could be seen, on certain clear days, from the roof of the building, where Frau Kopfman went to dry her hair and hang out their clothes. From this roof Hyman Kopfman could see a great park, such as they had at home in Vienna, and in the winter he could hear the ore boats honking on the lake. In spring he could hear the ice cracking up.

Was that Hyman Kopfman's story? If it was, it didn't add up to much. Nor did it seem to gain in the lengthy retelling, night after night. The facts were always the same: Hyman Kopfman had been born, without much reason, in Vienna, and in Chicago he had taken to wearing his father's fancy clothes. As his father had been something of a dandy Hyman Kopfman wore jackets with black satin lapels, shirts with celluloid cuffs and collars, pearl-gray spats, French braces, and patent leather shoes. Not that it mattered, since he never went down to the street. He spent day and night in the apartment where he walked from room to room, or with the silver-headed cane he might step into the hall. Concealed in the shaft of the cane was a sword, and when he stepped into the dim gaslit hallway, Hyman Kopfman would draw out the sword and fence with the dancing shadow of himself.

Ha! the Colonel would say, being an old swordsman, but Hyman Kopfman had shot his bolt. He could do no more than wag his feeble wrist in the air. His gums would bleed, his goatlike eyes would glow in a disturbing manner, but it was clear that even fencing with his shadow had been too much for him. Nothing had really happened. The Colonel doubted that anything ever would.

And then one day—one day just in passing—Hyman Kopfman raised his small head from his hand and said that the one thing he missed, really missed, that is, was the daily walk in the blind garden.

In the what? the Colonel said, as he thought he had missed the word.

In the blind garden, Hyman Kopfman replied. Had he somehow overlooked that? Hadn't he told the Colonel about the blind garden?

The Colonel, a cigarette in his mouth, had wagged his head.

At the back of the building there had been a small walled garden, Hyman Kopfman went on, a garden with gravel paths, shady trees, and places to sit. Men and women who were blind came there to walk. There were also flowers to smell, but they couldn't see them of course.

Well, well—the Colonel had replied, as he thought he now had the key to the story. One of the Kopfmans was blind, and Hyman Kopfman was ashamed to mention it. What difference did it make what Hyman Kopfman wore if his brother Paul, for instance, couldn't see him, and if Paul was blind he would hardly care how he looked himself. What difference did it make if he wore his mother's skirts around the house?

Your brother Paul was blind then—? the Colonel said.

Blind? said Hyman Kopfman, and blinked his own big eyes. Who said Paul was blind?

You were just saying—the Colonel replied.

From the window—interrupted Hyman Kopfman—what he saw below was like a tiny private park. There were trees along the paths, benches in the shade where the blind could sit. The only thing you might notice was how quiet and peaceful it was. Nobody laughed. The loud voices of children were never heard. It was the absence of children that struck Hyman Kopfman, as he was then very young himself, and liked to think of a park like that as a place for children to play. But the one below the window was not for bouncing balls, nor rolling hoops. No one came to this park to fly a kite, or to skip rope at the edge of the gravel, or to play a game of hide-and-seek around the trees. In fact there was no need, in a park like that, to hide from anyone. You could be there, right out in the open, and remain unseen. It was Paul Kopfman who pointed out that they might as well go down and sit there, as nobody would know whether they were blind or not. Nobody would notice that Hyman Kopfman was wearing celluloid cuffs and pearl-gray spats, or that Paul Kopfman was wearing a skirt and a peasant blouse. Nobody would care, down there, if their clothes were out of date, or that when Hyman Kopfman talked his wax-colored gums were inclined to bleed. It was the talking that made him excited, and the excitement that made his gums bleed, but down there in the garden he was not excited, and nobody cared. There were always flowers, because nobody picked them. There were birds and butterflies, because nobody killed them. There were no small boys with rocks and sticks, nor big boys with guns. There was only peace, and his brother Paul sat on the wooden benches talking with the women, as he didn't seem to care how old, and strange, and ugly they were. In some respects, he might as well have been blind himself.

How long did this go on—? the Colonel said, as he knew it couldn't go on forever. Nothing out of this world, nothing pleasant like that, ever did.

Well, one day his brother Otto—Hyman Kopfman said—his brother Otto put his head out the window and . . .

Never mind—! said the Colonel, and leaned forward as if to shut him up. He wagged his hand at the wrist, and the blue vein on his forehead crawled from his hair.

A man like you, Hyman Kopfman said, an old soldier, a Colonel, a man with gold medals—

Never mind! the Colonel had said, and took from the table his silver lighter, holding it like a weapon, his arm half-cocked, as if ready to throw.

Was Hyman Kopfman impressed? Well, he just sat there: he didn't go on. He smiled, but he didn't repeat what Otto had said. No, he just smiled with his bleeding gums, then raised the pale blue stump of his leg, sighted down the shinbone, pulled the trigger, and said *Bang!* He was like that. He didn't seem to know how hopeless he was.

For example, this Kopfman had only one foot but he sent out both of his shoes to be polished: he had only one arm, but he paid to have both sleeves carefully pressed. In the metal locker at the foot of his bed hung the pin-stripe suit with the two pair of pants, one pair with left leg neatly folded, and pinned to the hip. Some people might ask if a man like that needed two pair of pants. It was strange behavior for a person who was dying day by day. Not that he wanted very much, really—no, hardly more than most people had—all he really seemed to want was the useless sort of life that the Colonel had lived. To have slept with a woman, to have fought in a war, to have won or lost a large or small fortune, and to have memories, before he died, to look back to. Somehow, Hyman Kopfman had picked up the facts, so to speak, without having had the fun. He always used the word "fun" as he seemed to think that was what the Colonel had had.

Night after night the Colonel listened to this as he played with his lighter, or smoked too much, but he said very little as he felt that Hyman Kopfman was very young. Not in years, perhaps, but in terms of the experience he should have had. His idea of fun was not very complicated. His idea of life being what it was, the Colonel found it hard to understand why he hadn't reached out and put his hands on it. But he hadn't. Perhaps this thing had always been in his blood. Or perhaps life in America had not panned out as he had thought. At the first mention of Chicago, Hyman Kopfman would wave his stubby arm toward the window, roll his eyes, and make a dry rattle in his throat. That was what he felt, what he seemed to think, about America. But there was nothing that he wanted so much as to be out there living in it.

The case of Hyman Kopfman was indeed strange, but not so strange, in some respects, as the case of the old

man in the bed on his right. The Colonel had been failing; now for no apparent reason he began to improve.
Now that Hyman Kopfman was there beside him—a
hopeless case if there ever was one—the Colonel's pulse
grew stronger, he began to eat his food. He sat propped
up in bed in the manner of a man who would soon be up.
He even gazed through the window like a man who
would soon be out. Here you had the Colonel, who had
nothing to live for, but nevertheless was getting better,
while Hyman Kopfman, who hungered for life, was getting worse. It didn't make sense, but that was how it was.
Not wanting to live, apparently, was still not wanting to
die. So the Colonel, day by day, seemed to get better in
spite of himself.

The very week that Hyman Kopfman took a turn for
the worse, the Colonel took that turn for the better that
led the doctor to suggest that he ought to get up and walk
around. Adjust himself, like a newborn babe, to his wob-
bly legs. So he was pushed out of the bed, and the terry-
cloth robe that hung for months, unused, in the locker,
was draped around his sloping shoulders and a pair of
slippers were put on his feet. In this manner he walked
the floor from bed to bed. That is to say he toddled, from
rail to rail, and the effort made the sweat stand on his
forehead and the blue vein crawl like a slug from his
thinning hair. But everybody in the ward stared at him
enviously. He could feel in their gaze the hope that he
would trip, or have a relapse. But at least they were
courteous on the surface, they remarked how much
stronger he was looking, and made flattering comments
on how well he carried himself. They spoke of how fine
he would soon look in his uniform. All this from perfect
strangers; but Hyman Kopfman, the one who had
spoken to him intimately, snickered openly and never
tired of making slurring remarks. He referred to the

Colonel's soft arms as chicken wings. He called attention to the unusual length of the Colonel's neck. Naturally, the accident that had nearly killed the Colonel had not widened his shoulders any, and there was some truth in the statement that he was neck from the waist up. Nor had the Colonel's wide bottom, like that of a pear, which seemed to hold his figure upright, escaped Hyman Kopfman's critical eye. Nor his feet, which were certainly flat for an army man. A less disillusioned man than the Colonel would have made an official complaint, or brought up the subject of Hyman Kopfman's two-pants suit. But he said nothing. He preferred to take it in his stride. One might even say that he seemed to wax stronger on it. It was this observation, among others, that upset Hyman Kopfman the most, and led him to say things of which he was later ashamed. It was simply too much, for a dying man, to see one getting well who had nothing to live for, and this spectacle always put him into a rage. It also considerably hastened his end. It became a contest, of sorts, as to whether the Colonel would get back on his feet before Hyman Kopfman lost another limb, or managed to die. In this curious battle, however, Hyman Kopfman's willpower showed to a great advantage, and he deteriorated faster than the Colonel managed to improve. He managed to die, quite decently in fact, during the night. A Saturday night, as it happened, and the Colonel was able to call his wife and ask her to bring a suitable floral offering when she came.

1954

The Rites of Spring

The old man and the boy got on the train at Omaha. They walked through the coach to the water cooler, where the old man let the boy take the seat near the window while he stood in the aisle picking his teeth with a match. He was a farmer, dressed in the suit held in reserve for Sundays and travel, but the stripe in the coat had disappeared from the knees of the pants. The bend at the knee gave him the look of a man who was crouching, but within the pants; for a man of his age he stood straight enough. His name was Gudger, and he was the father of eight or ten kids, he wasn't sure which. In the state of Texas, where he had a farm, it didn't seem to matter.

The boy's name was Everett, but nobody ever called him that. His mother had called him Candy, but she was now dead. As his father was also dead there were people who referred to him as the orphan, while others, like the old man, referred to him as the little tyke. "What's going to be done about the little tyke?" the old man had said. As nobody seemed to know, the old man was taking him home to Texas where another little tyke wouldn't matter so much.

Since the boy had never been to Texas, nor out of Omaha for that matter, he kept his face pressed to the window, looking for it. As time passed he realized it must be far away. Every hour or so the old man told him that. "Don't git in such a hurry," the old man would say, and when the boy turned his head he might ask him, "How'd you like to butcher a hog?" The boy didn't know. But the old man was pleased at the thought of it. He would blink his pale, watery eyes and feel about in the air over his head for the wide-brimmed hat he had already taken off. It was there in his lap, with the ticket stubs sticking up in the band.

In the evening the old man took from his bag three hardboiled eggs he had brought from Texas, cracked them on the chair arm, peeled them, and gave one to the boy. The other two he ate himself. Later he slept, snoring into the hat he had placed over his face, but with one heavy hand on the boy's knee as if to hold him there. It led the boy to reflect that losing a father had not been so much. Losing a mother, however, was another thing, and it also troubled the boy to know that he was now in Oklahoma but none the wiser for it. He kept himself awake, however, just to breathe the night air. It seemed to him colder, just as the darkness seemed more black.

Under the lights on the station platform he looked for cowboys, for Indians, and where the streetlamps swung over empty corners he looked for tracks. Those that went off into the darkness single file.

It was still not light when they arrived in Texas and sat in a café, eating hotcakes, and looked at the red flares burning along the tracks. The old man spoke to the man behind the counter about the hog. He said he hoped he had got back in time to help butcher it. Then he went off for his team to the livery stable and the boy stood at the window, facing Texas, and watching the daylight come slowly along the tracks. Nothing but space seemed to be out there beyond the flares. Right there in the street were the railroad yards with the pale flares still hissing, but beyond the yards, off there where a hog was about to be butchered, the sky went up like a wall and the world seemed to end. The boy didn't like it. Something about it troubled him.

When the old man came with the buggy and the team of lean mares with the fly-net harncss, the boy wanted to ask just where they were going. Would a team of old mares ever get them there? Here he was, at the end of his journey according to what it said on his ticket, but he felt in his stomach that his travels had just begun. From the rise where the buggy rocked over the tracks he could see that the road went off toward somewhere, but that it also trembled, and began to blur like a ribbon of smoke. "Buggy needs greasin'—"he heard the old man say, but the boy hardly noticed the creaking, as it seemed such a small sound in such a big world. In the soft road dust the wheels were quiet, and the lapping sound of the reins, on the rumps of the mares, was like water running under the wheels.

As the boy had never looked upon the sea, nor any body of water he couldn't see over, he had no word for the landscape that he faced. The land itself seemed to roll like the floors in amusement parks. Without seeming to climb they would be on a rise with the earth gliding away before them, and in the faraway hollow there were towns a day's ride away. The wheels turned, the earth seemed to flow beneath the buggy, like dirty water, but nothing else changed and they seemed to be standing still. Here and there white-faced cattle, known as Herefords, stood in rows along the barbed-wire fence as if they had never seen a buggy, a horse, or a small boy before. They were always still there, as if painted on the fence, whenever he turned and looked. Then the road itself came to an end and they followed the wavering lines in the grass that the wheels had made the week before, on their way out. And when they came within sight of the farm—it seemed to recede, and they seemed to stalk it—the boy knew that he was nearing the rim of the world. What would he see when he peered over it? The hog. The hog seemed to be part of it. But the bleak house, with the boarded windows, was like a caboose left on a siding, and behind this house the world seemed to end. In the yard was a tree, but it would be wrong to say that the house and the tree stood on the sky, or that the body of the hog, small as it appeared, was dwarfed by it. The hog hung from the tree like some strange bellied fruit. Swarming about it in the yard were large boys with knives, sharpened pieces of metal, and small boys with long spears of broken glass. They all attacked the hog, hooting like Indians, and used whatever they had in hand to shave the stiff red bristles from the hog's hide. As the team of mares drew the buggy alongside, the boy could see a small hole, like a third eye, in the center of the hog's dripping head. The mouth was curved in a smile as if the swarm of boys scraping his hide tickled him.

"Guess we made it in time," the old man said, and using the crop of the buggy whip he tapped on one of the blood-smeared pails in the yard. A black cloud of flies rose into the air, then settled again. They made a sound as if the roaring wind had been siphoned into a bottle, leaving the yard empty and the flies trapped inside. If disturbed, they pelted the sides of the pail like a quick summer rain.

From his seat in the buggy—nobody called to him, or seemed to know that he was there—the boy watched the preparations for the butchering of the hog. A tall woman with a dough-colored face built a fire in the yard. There seemed to be no flesh on her lean body, and the dress she wore flapped in the wind as if hung from a hanger, or put out to dry on the line. Drawn low on her head was a stocking cap, and the stick with which she sometimes probed the fire was crooked like the handle of a witch's broom. Now and then a cloud of steam arose from the hog as a bucket of hot water was thrown on his body, or a puff of smoke, like a signal, arose from the fire. Now that the hog was shaved, the small boys carried wood, others put a new edge on the blades of their knives that had been dulled shaving him. An oil drum was carried from the house, and placed on the ground beside the fire, and over the fire a large sheet of metal, making it a stove. The cutting of the hog began when the metal plate was hot. The old man worked from the ground up, first cutting off the feet at the knuckle, the white knuckle showing like the milky eye of a blind horse. After the legs, he removed, carefully, the huge head. It was placed to one side, propped up in a pail, and although the hog's eyes were closed, it might be said that he attended his own barbecue. The smile was still on his face, as if he had long looked forward to it.

The light from the fire was like a coke burner on the greasy faces of the Gudger boys, but not the one who still sat in the buggy, out of the wind. The old man had spread the lap rug over him, and left him there. There was a lot going on, and a small city boy might get in the way. As he had eaten no pork his face was clean, but the smell of it was thick in his head and the shifting wind blew the savory smoke over him. At his back, when he turned to look, the state of Texas lay under the moon, the thick matted grass the leaden color of a dead sea. The house was an ark adrift upon it. Here and there, in the hollow of a wave or on a rise that appeared to be moving, lights would sparkle as if the sky were upside down. Behind him he could hear the crackling of the fire, and beyond the fire, strung up as if lynched, he could see the pale, strangely luminous body of the hog. But the great head, with the creased smiling eyes, still seemed to be amused at the proceedings, and gazed at the scene in the manner of the boy. And it was this head, with its de-tached air, the upper lip curled back as if grinning, that led the boy to feel that he and the hog had something in common. He and the hog, so to speak, had both lost something. In each case they had given up more than what remained. The boy wondered how it was, in this situation, that the hog could look on the scene with what appeared to be a smile of amusement. The joke seemed to be, if he could believe the hog, on everybody else. On the cursing old man with the sweating face, on his dough-colored wife, on his family of kids who stood around the fire, their faces oily with the hog himself. But when the boy closed his eyes to think about this he saw the grinning face of the hog before him, and the third small eye, in the middle of his forehead, seemed to wink. The fat that splattered in the fire crackled like burning twigs.

The cooking of the hog went on through the night. Small slices of the pork, no larger than a dollar, were dropped to fry on the metal sheet, and the fat ran off into the oil drum at the side. Into the fat the crisp slices of the pork were dropped. The drum filled up, in this way, layer by layer. When the fire died down the body of the hog would appear to recede into the shadows, then it would come forward, like a ghost, when the flames flared up. There was always less hog when the boy turned to look.

In the cool of the night the dough-faced woman sometimes leaned over the fire for warmth, or stirred, with her pointed stick, the dying bed of coals. Something about it raised the small hairs on the boy's neck. It also brought, as it did to the hog, a smile to his face. The moonlit scene, the pale-faced butchers, the ghostly body of the hog, and the great milky emptiness of the night seemed bewitched. More was going on than met the eye, but according to the hog, it was not serious. The boy and the hog both knew this, but nobody else.

Toward morning the fire died down, and the faint honking of geese woke the boy up. He saw their dark wavering arrow on the morning sky. There was no longer noise around the fire, or the sound of hot fat spilling into the barrel, and when the boy raised his head he saw that he was alone with the head and the two great hams that hung from the tree. Whether the head still smiled or not was hard to say. It was still there in the pail, gazing up at the now moonless sky, the small black hole between the eyes like an ornament. Somewhere to the east, blown thin on the wind, a rooster crowed. The lonely sound troubled the boy as it meant another day, no better than the last one, was about to begin. Very likely the head of the hog, and the smile, would be cut up next. The ears would be made, as he had heard some-

171

where, into a purse. His feet would be put into barrels and sold in Omaha. His curly tail would make a tassel at the end of a whip. Everything would be used, nothing would remain, and thinking of that the boy sat up in the buggy. On the pale morning sky he could see the rope that strung up the hams. This rope had been tied to a post in the yard, but it had been loosened from time to time in order to lower the hog's shrinking body. He had seen how this was done. Even a city boy might learn the knack of it. He climbed from the buggy, using the spokes like rungs of a ladder, and as he loosened the rope he wrapped the coils around his waist. He had seen this done by the fat man in a tug of war. It was hard to say what he had in mind, if anything. He unraveled the rope until the great hams, taking up the slack with a snap, swept him from the ground like a dummy and swung him in a wide arc. The jolt had drawn the coils at his waist, and he hung like a sack, bent like a jackknife, and the blurred movement of the earth sweeping past made him close his eyes. As he swung, the wind gave him a clockwise turn. His fingers swelled thick, and he could feel the pulse when he closed his hands. On the east rim of the world, like light beneath a door, the dawn lit up the faces of both the boy and the hog, who appeared to be exchanging secretive smiles at all they had seen.

1952

172

The Cat's Meow

What were the symptoms?

No voice. A total loss of voice. Using a small pocket flash, with an intense white beam, Dr. Payne peered into the patient's throat. "Some redness," he said, and appeared to relax.

"Some redness?" Morgan repeated.

"Laryngitis. Not uncommon, you know. Does he eat?"

Oh yes, he ate very well. One might say too well. Dr. Payne turned away to make jottings on his 3 × 5 file card. There were two cards for the patient, both sides recording his history.

"Twice a day," said Dr. Payne, tapping pills from a jar, and counting out twelve he slipped them into a packet. They were moderate size pills, pink in color. Both Morgan and the patient disliked large pills. Morgan wondered if their taste was minty. "If there's no improvement by Friday—" Dr. Payne continued, but Morgan was sure there would be marked improvement. The patient had never been long silent. Besides, there were twelve pills, and only a small redness. The patient, a large, fat, short haired cat (the card recorded his weight at 17 pounds 4 oz.) mewed silently, his motor purring. Morgan turned to see if Dr. Payne had observed it. A most curious effect. "Hmmmmmm—" said Dr. Payne.

"Thought it was my hearing, first time I heard it—I mean *saw* it," said Morgan. "Gave me quite a start."

Dr. Payne smiled. He used the ballpoint pen he was holding to scratch the skull of the patient, which seemed to please him.

"How come," asked Morgan, "you can hear his motor running, but no voice?"

Dr. Payne was long accustomed to ridiculous questions from non-patients. "This one is Bloom, right?"

"This is Bloom," replied Morgan. Hearing his name, hearing it from Morgan, Bloom lifted his tail and soundlessly meowed. Why was that so disturbing?

"Makes for quiet, I must say!" said Dr. Payne.

Actually it did not make for quiet. It made for silence.

"The big problem is the morning," said Morgan. "He comes to the door about five, give or take a few minutes. I *know* he's there, but I can't hear him. A strain for both of us."

"You complain about that?" Dr. Payne was clearing up for the next patient. A calico type cat with glassy, rheum-clouded eyes crouched in a cage at the door to the lobby. Morgan hoped it wasn't catching. Over nine years

Bloom had had many things, but no trouble with his eyes. About the soundless meow, it had ceased to be a pleasure when it became a worry. He had relied on that meow, as he did his wife's breathing. If for any reason she checked that breathing, in order to listen to something, he was awake in an instant. In the past week his sleep had been disturbed by the tick of the clock that had replaced the cat's meow. Even the luminous numerals on its face interfered with his sleep. At five o'clock sharp, give or take a few minutes, he would get up and find Bloom at the bedroom door. Morgan could not hear it, but he could sense the puzzled irritation in the cat's manner.

"If I were you," said Dr. Payne, "I'd enjoy it while it lasts. It won't be long."

Into his traveling box, with its wire-mesh top, Morgan pushed the reluctant Bloom. A marvelous cat. Reluctant but seldom stubborn. If Morgan said so, he would do it. Absolute, unerring faith in Morgan, in all for the best.

Outside the clinic, in the seat of the car, he knew that Bloom was silently mewing. He did not like cars. If he had eaten first, he always whooped it up. But what a relief it had seemed, driving over, not to hear his yawping complaint. Not a meow at all, of the usual sort, but a sound squeezed up from his innards. Now Morgan missed it. To hear nothing at all was worse.

These trips to the clinic Morgan made alone after a disastrous worming session. His wife, Charlotte, had never once imagined that they were in Bloom's stomach, and would come up the front way. It had been too much. Charlotte had disappeared into the ladies' room of the Texaco station.

Morgan and Charlotte, Bloom and Pussy-baby, lived in a hillside house under a cluster of live oaks, a heaven for cats. On the two-thirds acre there were too many birds, foolish, stupid little birds scratching under the bushes, and there were too many creatures better left unnamed that could be heard, at dawn, plaintively shrieking, but Morgan had explained (he had lied, to put it bluntly) that cats were quick and merciful killers. Without cats, he soberly warned her, the place would suffer a population explosion, and Morgan had only to mention the word rodent to confuse her sympathies toward mice.

The other cat, Pussy-baby, a small black Manx, had a card at the clinic almost free of afflictions. He had had his shots, and he had once been wormed, but otherwise even bugs could not keep an eye on him. A tiny fawnlike creature, he had also eluded a determined search for a suitable name. He had been a baby, a pussy-baby, and after several years of futile experiments, plain names, weird names, and just plain cute names, he remained Pussy-baby. Fortunately, this was only a problem when he met people, which was seldom, or had to go along with Bloom to the clinic, where the girl at the desk, looking for his card, would cry out in the lobby, "Which one is Pussy-baby?" Charlotte had steeled herself to endure it. Morgan would stand near the door thumbing the pages of a magazine. Pussy-baby was Charlotte's cat.

In being ten weeks younger than Bloom, Pussy-baby's life and times had been predetermined. The big loutish Bloom, a friend to man, *any* man, and most women, at the sight of Pussy-baby had been transformed into a cunning, jungle tiger. Quite possibly, lacking experience, he failed to recognize the creature as a fellow cat. Batlike ears, button eyes. A startled look or no look at all. In the first few weeks Bloom had mauled him, pounced on him, carried him about like a homeless kitten, until the problem had been partially solved by concealing him beneath food cartons. One can well imagine—Charlotte

176

always says—what Morgan would have been like after such a childhood. At dawn, with Bloom, Pussy-baby leaves the house to lie concealed under something, or peer down from something, occasionally returning to gulp food from the saucer in the kitchen, to reappear at dusk, as the lights come on, and assume his role as a member of the family, crouching like a sphinx on Morgan's knee, which is well scarred by his claws, or curling up with the dreaded Bloom for a snooze, or a bout of face washing. Another cat? One has to believe it. Wild rather than tame, murderous claws, inflexible tastes, indifferent alike to threats and persuasions, given to swallowing string, choking on grass, and sneaking into the garage when Morgan has his back turned. There he hides until late at night, when his penetrating mew, like an out-of-order buzzer, is instantly heard by Charlotte. There is nothing to be done, of course, but rescue him. He was once gone and given up for lost over a long Labor Day weekend, but when it was over, and the neighbors had returned, he was found in the cab of the Steyerhausers' pickup, the leather palms of a pair of garden gloves gnawed away. Morgan tirelessly wants to know what earthly good such a cat is, and Charlotte tirelessly reminds him what a cat is good for is a cat's business. There are moments, however, somewhat infrequent, in no conceivable way to be relied on, when Pussy-baby will pause, as if petrified, as he crosses a room or enters the kitchen, holding a posture only seen in the low reliefs of creatures and birds on Egyptian temples. A captured moment of time! It might last a full minute, neither Morgan nor Charlotte breathing, then the merest twitch of his stub tail would indicate the time-destroyer, life itself, once again circulating in his tiny veins, starting up his motor so that he could pick up from where he had stopped. Charlotte and Morgan are agreed that these

177

moments almost justify his endless exasperations, and that if cats were as rare as diamonds people would pay more money for them. What good is it for Morgan to remind her that they are not?

Back at the house, Morgan stands with Bloom in the grass at the edge of the driveway, on the chance that he might have something on his mind. It had been Bloom's decision that he was Morgan's cat, both of them being outdoor types fond of peeing while the sprinklers are running. What can Charlotte do? *Her* cat is Pussy-baby, but there are times even Charlotte loses patience. Food mostly. Both cats will eat *any*thing found in the yard, but absolutely *nothing* from the table. If it is on the table, and they find it, that of course is another matter. It distresses Charlotte that after nine years Pussy-baby would rather cheat than not cheat. If he turns up his nose at the chopped kidney, just leave the can on the counter and he will gulp it. The look he gives Charlotte, licking his chops, is that he might turn on her next. That is too much: but nevertheless, that is how he is. If Morgan lets drop that such an independent cat should *really* be independent, Charlotte will accuse him of not liking cats unless they are willing to do his bidding, and were not really cats at all, but some new kind of dog. It is a fact that Bloom, since he was a kitten, either thinks that Morgan is a special kind of cat, or has very uncatlike characteristics, tailing Morgan, relaxing with Morgan, driving Charlotte crazy in Morgan's absence, as if she, Charlotte, had hidden Morgan in a closet, locked him in the garage, or possibly worse. His voice and his manner on such occasions is unmistakably hostile, which is hard to believe in such an easygoing, affectionate fat cat. Both Morgan and Bloom appreciate that Morgan and Bloom are pretty unusual, but tactful in the area of making any ridiculous claims. If Morgan snaps his fingers, Bloom sometimes comes, other times he does not.

The rear view of Bloom being one of Morgan's favorites—a fat trousered harem master—they walk in tandem, Bloom leading, his tail erect and his button gleaming from the attention received in the clinic office. Charlotte stands at the door, waiting, relieved to see that the patient is walking.

"You wouldn't believe it," said Morgan. "Laryngitis."

He was right, she does not believe it. Morgan is a joker, and his jokes cost him the desired effects of a true story. Charlotte impatiently waits.

"I'm not joking," he reports. "It's laryngitis."

Passing Charlotte, Bloom glanced up to soundlessly meow, then enter the house. Charlotte followed him without comment. When Morgan insisted on his little jokes, there was nothing for Charlotte to do but wait. In the kitchen, at the patio door, she lifted and rattled the box of Friskies. Bloom soundlessly meowed. She spilled a handful into his bowl, the one farthest from the wall, where his tail would not catch in the heavy, sliding patio door. With Pussy-baby there was no problem.

"Payne gave me some pills," said Morgan. "He says it ought to clear up by the weekend."

They stand watching Bloom crunch up his Friskies. The big, loutish cat is very delicate in his eating habits. In contrast, the fawnlike Pussy-baby covers his face and the floor when he laps milk, bolts hunks of liver, whoops up half-and-half.

This little jaunt to the clinic, going and coming, plus a twenty-minute wait for Dr. Payne, has raised hell with Morgan's working schedule. He is a writer. From nine to one he sits at his desk. He leaves the packet of pills for Bloom on the counter, then walks through the house to his study. The desk lamp shines on the sheet of paper in his typewriter. Three lines have been typed. One of the

179

lines has been canceled. To get back to where he was, to recover his thought, Morgan takes the last sheet typed from the wire basket. Near its center is a smear that has dried, to which a few black hairs are attached. Other things being equal, the hours of nine to one Bloom spends in Morgan's wire basket. That is how it has been for some years now. It is how things are. Sheets are added to the basket when he leaves for a snack, or when Morgan lifts him and slips them beneath him, accepted by Bloom as an important part of the morning's work. On occasion so little work is accomplished, and the basket sits so close to the typewriter carriage, that Bloom naps with his chin on the nob and work is further delayed until something disturbs him. On some occasions it is Morgan. The cat faces him, his eyes blinking in the desk light, and the look he gives Morgan, and Morgan returns, is not something to be lightly dealt with, or even when soberly and thoughtfully dealt with, put into words. The cat is the first to speak, and Morgan replies. There is a passage in a book by Konrad Lorenz that Morgan has read to Charlotte, concerned with the habits and cackling of the Greylag goose. While the geese are strolling about, or grazing, the mated pair keep in touch by cackling, which had been translated to mean "Here am I, where are you?" Cats meowed, geese cackled, people talked. Morgan didn't want to make too much of this, but neither did he want to make too little, having shared his life, and his wire basket, with Bloom. While he had his voice he said plainly to Morgan, "Here I am!" and expected an answer.

Morgan read the last sheet, returned it to the basket, then sat for something less than a full minute waiting for the cat to come from the kitchen. He came, as usual, to the side of the desk, where the light narrowed the pupils of his eyes to slits, and reminded Morgan of the lizards in his past. Acknowledging the patient's need for special treatment, Morgan stopped to lift the seventeen pounds of cat to his place in the wire basket. It was customary for Bloom to thank him for that, but this time he said nothing.

A few summers back, a big orange tiger with the gait of a leopard, and huge white paws, liked the patio and decided to adopt them. Morgan himself was all for a *maison à trois*—what was another mouth to feed? The handsome tiger had beautiful manners and elegant disdain for the dumbfounded Bloom. In the morning he would sidle through the patio door, eat Pussy-baby's chopped liver, share Bloom's Friskies. If Bloom left the house, there he was on the patio lounge. Morgan was at the sink, squeezing oranges, when the blood-curdling shrieking made the hairs on his neck rise. In the clearing between two fuchsia bushes—a scene they transformed into a jungle—the two big cats stood eye to eye, horribly growling, the mouth of Bloom tufted with orange hair, the mouth of the tiger with black hair, the bell-like flowers rocking wildly from the whiplike snap of their tails. In a ballet leap, they went up together, legs thrashing, then fell with a thud that Morgan actually felt in the floor. Pure fury. A spectacle both appalling, terrifying, and gratifying. In helpless shame Morgan let it go on, enthralled by the unleashing of such forces. Then he used the sink spray to douse them, which they appeared to enjoy as a cooler, before he ran to the hose at the side of the house and let them have it full blast. The tiger had to be carted to another county, where adoptions were less complicated, and Bloom had to be driven to the clinic for what was listed on the bill as surgery. Dr. Payne thought it amazing how well he had recovered. At his age (roughly sixty-three, as calculated by Charlotte) Bloom was now kept in the house until dawn to avoid further confrontations.

After giving Bloom his pill, Morgan and Charlotte went out to dinner with friends and were late getting home. It was customary for Bloom to step out for a moment, but he slept on. If there was something in the pill to put him to sleep, Morgan should have taken one of them himself. Worried about Bloom, they had ignored Pussy-baby who had cunningly made his way into the bedroom, where the noise he made, licking his coat, was like that of an animal chewing up his neighbor. Morgan had to switch on the light to find him in the half-open drawer of the bedside table. In the top drawer he kept a loaded pistol, wrapped in a cloth scented with furniture polish. On sleepless nights, like this one, Morgan tried to recall the exact nature of its operation. He had never actually fired it. When he bought the gun he meant to drive into the mountains and shoot it a few times, just to get the feel of it, but Charlotte would not allow the pistol in the car knowing there was a law against transporting handguns. Who were the people who were always getting shot? People fooling with guns.

Morgan's restlessness was due in part to the rich food —Charlotte's friend was a disciple of Julia Child—in part to his persistent feeling that Bloom was at the door —or at some door. There were three doors he used to enter or exit the house: the one to the patio, which was customary, the chained and bolted front door, which was a damn nuisance, and in unpredictable emergencies, the door to the deck. The deck door, as a rule, was an IN door—bad weather, large dogs, garbage trucks, meter readers—and in practical terms it was Charlotte's business. Morgan let the cats out—Charlotte let them in. Charlotte could hear the faint mew of Pussy-baby, at the door to the deck: Morgan swore he could not. If Morgan lied on this point, or stretched it a little, it was in the interest of law and order. Disturbed by a break in the routine (the sight of Morgan) Pussy-baby might take off instead of coming in. Leave well enough alone, was Morgan's rule, if it applied to cats.

This early morning, however—it was not yet four—he knew the cat, Bloom, was at the door, wanting out. It was not his usual time, but it had been an unusual day. To check on this impression Morgan went to the door, and there he was, silhouetted against the nightlight, his *back* to Morgan by way of indicating his irritation at Morgan's slowness. In tandem, Morgan trailing, they padded through the house to the patio door, where the cat made his cautious, sniffing exit. The night air chill in his lungs, and pleasurably cool on his body, Morgan might stand there until his feet were cold, sharing something of the cat's experience, the sensation of leaving a safe haven for the dark, watchful jungle of the night. The cat in Morgan at one with Morgan in the cat.

It was not unheard-of for Morgan, if he couldn't sleep, to let the cat out and then make himself some coffee, as if he meant to start the day early. He might read the morning paper, or sit there watching the sky get light. Bloom came back into the house when Morgan stepped out to empty the garbage. He was in the wire basket, curled up asleep, when Morgan left the house to turn on the sprinklers. He used the patio door, walking around the house—this little tour might take him four or five minutes—to get to the sprinkler faucet under the deck. The cat, Bloom, sat in the shelter of the deck, his customary place.

"How did this cat get here so quick?" he called to Charlotte.

"He meowed at the deck door," she replied.

"He what?"

There was a pause. "I just know I heard him meow," said Charlotte. Morgan was delighted. He stooped to stroke Bloom and praise him for his quick recovery. Bloom accepted this interest without comment.

"You sure he meowed?"

"How would I know he was there?" replied Charlotte. She had been in the bathroom, the door standing open. Even with the water running she had heard him.

This sort of thing with Bloom—never with Pussy-baby—was frequently a subject for discussion. It always amused Charlotte the way that Bloom, asleep in his chair, would know when Morgan had left the room, allow him one long minute to return, then immediately go in search of him. Was it feline ESP? Morgan didn't really think so. It was just like man, of course, to call it *extrasensory* if he didn't have it himself. It was simply that Bloom heard what he wanted to hear, and nothing else. The slightest move that Morgan made he picked up on his radar. Hadn't they both noticed how his ears tuned in even while he napped? With the house full of people, all of them yakking, Bloom would hear the drop of a Friskie in the kitchen, or the tap of a bird's beak in the feedbox on the deck. If Charlotte or Morgan were attuned like that the world would be a different place than they found it, and quieter. As for what Charlotte had heard, in his afflicted condition Bloom might well make a noise one time, and not another. Morgan did not feel that the time was ripe to make an issue about it. He turned off the sprinklers, then went for the mail, a chore that Bloom observed from the top of the driveway. When he glanced up from the street the cat was gone—or perhaps he should say, not visible. From the shrubs on the left Pussy-baby, with his tailless, uncatlike canter, saw him to the house along the walk at the side, then took off like an escort who had done his duty. The fat cat Bloom was in the basket on his desk, tidying up.

Morgan went to bed early, to catch up on lost sleep, and did very well to the moment he awakened, as if called. At his side, Charlotte's rhythmical exhalation was like the wash of water in a bed of reeds. Morgan was wide-awake, but without apprehension, as if he had been awakened by a familiar alarm. He felt the peace of one who, having been chosen, was spared a choice. After a few moments of this he went to the door, the curtains stirring as it opened. At full aperture not even the eyes of the cat were visible. But at the touch of the fingers Morgan extended he turned to leave, once more clearly expressing his irritation. "Cat got your tongue?" Morgan hissed at him, this being one of his little jokes. From Bloom no comment. At the patio door Morgan restrained the impulse to give him a powerful assist from the rear, Bloom pausing on the threshold, eyes lidded, to gingerly sniff the night air.

Back in bed he lay awake for sometime, thanks to the caterwauling beneath the window. The cats were in good voice, and not to be rushed. One voice seemed more familiar to Morgan than the other, even shriller for want of practice. Was it unusual for a cat to lose his normal speech, but still be able to howl? Ordinarily Morgan would have leaped from the bed to throw the empty tin cans (kept there for that purpose) to where they would roll the length of the concrete driveway, arousing the Steyerhauser dog to a frenzy of barking that often silenced the cats. Now he just lay there, however, until Charlotte leaped from the bed to clap her hands on the windowsill, then shriek "Bloom! Bloom! Bloom!" as if part of a cheer. This considerable racket was followed by a silence in which they could both hear a plaintive meowing at the door to the deck. Lost in the mists of time were the reasons why Morgan let the cats out and Charlotte let them in. Now he could hear her, he could hear *them*—Pussy-baby also having entered—while she refilled their bowl of Friskies, then padded back through the house to tell him, knowing he was awake and listening, that dear, darling old Bloom, thanks to the scuffle, had recovered his voice. It was too bad that included his howl, but in these matters one couldn't be choosy, as Morgan knew.

It still proved to be early, but having once been out, Bloom was usually content to stay in. Charlotte slept like a baby, but Morgan was not free of the impression that a cat, the non-meowing Bloom, was back at the door. It could be nothing more than Morgan's apprehension, resulting from the patient's laryngitis; it could be, but Morgan was reasonably sure it was not. The presence of Bloom, his radar beaming, was there on the grid of Morgan's mind. As plain as day, when days were plain, Morgan recorded the message *Here I am—where the hell are you?* Taking care not to disturb Charlotte's sleep Morgan tiptoed to the door, opened it gently, and stooped to stroke the invisible cat. There he was, his motor purring as he arched his back. They then proceeded as usual to the patio door, when the first touch of dawn blazed on the glass: the whine of freeway traffic had displaced the music of the spheres. Morgan might have preferred a more orthodox alliance—this one was sure to cost him much sleep—but in the nature of things he could see no reason why one creature, in union with another, through affliction and affection, in sickness and in health, should not dispense with the obvious. Turning to give him a look, not a meow, Bloom took his leave.

1975

186